HARLEQUIN *Presents*

2133
October

Anne Mather

INNOCENT SINS

D0034438

HARLEQUIN®
Makes any time special ™

"Are you afraid you won't be able to trust yourself with me?"

Laura's jaw dropped. "In your dreams," she muttered, turning away, and although Oliver knew he was being all kinds of a fool for prolonging this, he reached out to her.

The vivid tangle of red-gold curls fell about her shoulders, and his throat constricted at the sight. She looked so young, so vulnerable, so much like the girl who'd come to his bedroom all those years ago. He'd wanted her then, and he wanted her now, no matter how stupid that might be.

Moving closer, Oliver let his hand slide to the back of her neck, under the warm folds of her robe. "You are afraid of me." His thumb massaged the skin below her ear. "You have no reason to be."

"Don't I?"

There was a curious note in her voice, but he refused to acknowledge it. "No," he said huskily. "I only want us to be—to be—"

"Friends?"

"Lovers…." he offered unsteadily.

ANNE MATHER has been writing since she was seven, but it was only when her first child was born that she fulfilled her dream of becoming a published author. Her first book, *Caroline,* met with immediate success, and since then, Anne has written more than 130 novels, reaching a readership that spans the world.

Born and raised in the north of England, Anne still makes her home there with her husband, two children and, now, grandchildren. Asked if she finds writing a lonely occupation, she replies that her characters always keep her company. In fact, she is so busy sorting out their lives that she often doesn't have time for her own! An avid reader herself, she devours everything from sagas and romances to suspense.

A *New York Times* bestselling author, Anne Mather has also seen one of her novels, *Leopard in the Snow,* turned into a movie.

Books by Anne Mather

HARLEQUIN PRESENTS®

2032—HER GUILTY SECRET
2055—THE BABY GAMBIT
2109—THE MILLIONAIRE'S VIRGIN

MIRA® BOOKS

DANGEROUS TEMPTATION

Anne Mather

INNOCENT SINS

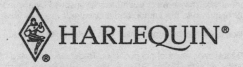

TORONTO • NEW YORK • LONDON
AMSTERDAM • PARIS • SYDNEY • HAMBURG
STOCKHOLM • ATHENS • TOKYO • MILAN • MADRID
PRAGUE • WARSAW • BUDAPEST • AUCKLAND

ISBN 0-373-12133-4

INNOCENT SINS

First North American Publication 2000.

Copyright © 2000 by Anne Mather.

Visit us at www.eHarlequin.com

Printed in U.S.A.

CHAPTER ONE

OLIVER could hear the phone ringing as he vaulted up the steps to the front door. Light shone out through the fan-shaped skylight above, illuminating the crisp piles of snow that he guessed Thomas had cleared earlier in the day. But although he was fairly sure his manservant was at home it seemed obvious that the old man was not going to answer the call.

Which pointed to the fact that he knew who it was. Which, in turn, led Oliver to believe it must be his mother. Only if Stella had been ringing fairly constantly all day would Thomas choose to ignore the summons. He and Stella had never liked one another, and the fact that his mother had expected her son to return yesterday morning would perhaps explain her eagerness to ask him about his trip.

Or not.

Oliver's mouth eased into a wry smile as he inserted his key in the lock. In his experience, Stella was seldom interested in anything that didn't immediately affect her, and if she had been ringing on and off all day there was probably something personal on her mind.

The warmth that accompanied the opening of the door was welcome. Oliver would have preferred not to return to London in the middle of one of the coldest spells of the winter. Particularly since he'd spent the last three weeks sweltering in the extreme heat of the Malaysian jungle.

'Mr Oliver!'

To his relief the phone stopped its shrill bleating at the same moment that Thomas Grayson appeared at the end of the long hallway that ran from front to back of the house. Although Oliver had tried to persuade the old man that such

5

formality wasn't necessary, Thomas insisted on addressing him that way.

Now Oliver hoisted the bag containing his camera equipment inside and, closing the door, leaned back against it for a moment's rest. He didn't often take the time to appreciate the elegant beauty of the narrow, four-storey Georgian house that was his home, but he was always relieved to find that nothing had changed in his absence.

'I expected you back yesterday, Mr Oliver.'

Thomas's tone was almost reproving and Oliver wondered if he considered he was to blame for the delay. 'The plane was late leaving Singapore, and there's been a snowstorm over western Europe for the past twenty-four hours, in case you hadn't noticed,' he responded drily. 'But, hey, don't let that worry you. And it's good to see you, too.'

Thomas, who had been about to wrest his employer's ruck-sack and garment bag from his hands, straightened abruptly. 'Oh, I'm sorry, Mr Oliver,' he said, with evident sincerity. 'Of course it's good to have you back. But—' He paused. 'I'm afraid there's been something of an emergency while you've been away.'

'What now?'

Oliver was wearily aware that he wasn't in the best mood to suffer another of his mother's crises, if that was what Thomas meant. Resignation replaced his earlier optimism. Where Stella was concerned, there were always emergencies, most recently occasioned by his mother's inability to live within the allowance Griff gave her.

'Your mother's been trying to reach you for the past forty-eight hours,' Thomas continued, and just for a moment Oliver wondered if Laura could be involved. His stepsister used to be a constant thorn in his mother's side, but she'd gone to live in the United States almost seven years ago now. 'I regret to have to tell you that your stepfather died two days ago,' Thomas added gently. 'Mrs Williams has been desperate to get in touch with you ever since.'

Oliver's resignation vanished. 'So that's why you refused to answer the phone?'

'Well, yes.' Thomas was defensive. 'Mrs Williams was getting rather—well, abusive. She accused me of not giving you her messages. She wouldn't believe that I didn't know where you were.'

Oliver pulled a wry face. He knew his mother must have said something upsetting for Thomas to ignore her calls at a time like this. 'If she'd rung the airline, she'd have found out why I was late,' he said wearily. He'd been travelling for the past forty-eight hours and he was tired. He'd been looking forward to nothing more exhausting than taking a hot shower and collapsing into bed. Now he was going to have to deal with his mother, and he could imagine how harrowing that was going to be.

'I'd better give her a ring,' he said, abandoning any hope of getting some rest. He picked up the bag containing his camera equipment and started up the stairs ahead of Thomas. 'Perhaps you'd repack the rucksack with some clean underwear. If I have to go down to Penmadoc, I might as well be prepared.'

'You're not proposing to drive down to Penmadoc tonight!' Thomas was horrified.

'I'll probably have no choice in the matter,' replied his employer, entering the lamplit room on his left at the top of the stairs. The first floor of the house was given over to this room, which was Oliver's study, the dining room, and a comfortable sitting room, with his bedroom suite and two guest suites on the second floor. He went straight to the wet bar to help himself to a small shot of whisky. 'I know, I know,' he groaned, when Thomas stood shaking his head in the doorway. 'But I need some fortification. I'll have a sandwich and some coffee before I leave, I promise.'

Thomas's disapproval was apparent, but in the eight years since he'd come to work for Oliver he'd learned when to back off. Leaving his employer to make his call, he continued on his way to the second floor and Oliver heard him opening and closing drawers and sliding hangers about in his dressing room.

The phone seemed to ring for a long time before anyone answered it. Oliver was beginning to wonder if his mother had guessed it was him and was paying him back for not being there when she needed him. It was the sort of thing Stella might do, only not at a time like this, surely.

He could imagine the sound echoing round the draughty old hall, with its beamed ceiling and uneven polished floor. He couldn't ever remember feeling warm at Penmadoc in the winter. Laura used to say the house was haunted and, when he was younger, he'd half believed her.

Laura...

'Penmadoc Hall.'

A voice with a strong Welsh accent interrupted his maundering. 'Oh, hello,' he said, putting the past behind him. 'This is Oliver Kemp. Is my mother there?'

'Oliver.' The tone was familiar to him now, and Eleanor Tenby was surprisingly amiable for once. 'Your mother will be pleased to hear from you. I'll get her for you.'

'Thanks.'

Oliver didn't attempt to detain her, even though it was unusual for Laura's aunt Nell to show any consideration towards either him or his mother. Had it not been for the fact that she was Maggie Williams' sister, and Penmadoc had always been her home, Stella would have got rid of her long ago. But, although Griff had indulged her in most things, where Eleanor was concerned, he wouldn't be moved.

And, ultimately, it had suited his mother to have a ready-made housekeeper, thought Oliver wryly. Because Laura's mother had been ill for several years before her death, Eleanor had taken over the running of the household from her. When Maggie died and Griff married again, Eleanor had retained her position. Stella might have grumbled at first, but she'd never been the kind of woman to enjoy domestic duties.

'Oliver?'

His mother's voice came shrilly over the wires, and although he was used to her dramatics by now Oliver sensed she was more than usually *distrait*. There was a note of hysteria there that he hadn't expected, and he prepared himself to comfort her as best he could.

'Hi, Ma,' he greeted her, with his usual irreverence. Then he said, gently, 'I was so sorry to hear the news about Griff. You must be shattered.'

'Yes. Yes, I am.' Stella's response was taut and uneven. 'Where the hell have you been, Oliver? I've been trying to reach you for days.'

'I know. Thomas told me.'

'Thomas!' His mother fairly spat the old man's name. 'That little weasel had the nerve to tell me that he didn't know how to reach you. As if you'd have gone away without leaving a forwarding address.'

Oliver heaved a deep breath. 'He wasn't lying, Ma. I left Singapore yesterday morning. But the plane was delayed with engine trouble in Bahrain, and then, what with the weather—'

'You could have phoned home.'

'Why?' Oliver could feel his sympathy dissolving into irritation. 'Thomas has eyes. He could see the problem the weather was creating for himself.'

'Is that a dig at me?'

Stella's voice wobbled a little now and Oliver realised that Griff's death had hit her even harder than he'd thought. He was more used to her complaining about the disadvantages of being married to a man considerably older than herself, who apparently didn't understand why she was perpetually short of funds.

'It's not a dig,' he said gently. 'Naturally, if I'd known about Griff—'

'Yes.' To his relief, his mother seemed to have herself in control again. 'Yes, well, I suppose that's a fair point. There didn't appear to be anything wrong with him when you went away, did there? How was any of us to know that in three weeks he'd be dead?' Her voice rose again, but she managed to steady it. 'You're coming down, of course?'

'Of course.' Oliver conceded to himself that there was no way he could avoid it. 'I'll get something to eat and then I'll be on my way.'

'Thank God!' Stella was obviously relieved and Oliver acknowledged the fact that so far as his mother was concerned his feelings counted for little. But then, he'd always known that, hadn't he? 'I'll wait up for you.'

She would have rung off then, but Oliver had to ask. 'Griff?' he said awkwardly. 'I mean—how did it happen?'

'He had a heart attack,' said Stella shortly, clearly not prepared to elaborate on the phone. 'Drive carefully.'

The line went dead and Oliver replaced his receiver with a troubled hand. A heart attack! As far as he knew, Griff had never had any problems with his heart. But what did he know? In the twenty years since Griff had married his mother, they'd hardly become bosom buddies, and although age had brought a certain understanding between them they'd never been really close.

There was still so much he wanted to know. Was Laura coming home for her father's funeral? Of course, she must be. She hadn't come home when her marriage to Conor Neill had foundered, but that was different. Her work was in New York. She'd made a niche for herself there. Why would she come back to England, or, more precisely, Wales, when she had a perfectly good job in the United States?

His lips twisted. Naturally, Stella had been relieved that she hadn't returned to Penmadoc. The last thing she'd wanted was for her stepdaughter to come back and form an alliance with her father against her. Oliver couldn't deny that Stella had always been jealous of the relationship Laura had had with her father. And Laura had never forgiven his mother for replacing Maggie less than a year after her mother's death.

'I've laid out some clean clothes in your bedroom, Mr Oliver.' Thomas spoke somewhat diffidently from the doorway, evidently cognisant of the disturbed expression his employer was wearing. 'I assume you'll be taking a shower before you leave?' he added. 'I'll have some coffee and a light meal ready when you come downstairs.'

Oliver flexed his shoulders. 'Just a sandwich, thanks,' he said wearily. 'I had something to eat on the plane, and I'm not really hungry.' He paused before saying gratefully, 'But the coffee would be welcome. Is there plenty of fuel in the car?'

'I expect you'll use the Jeep?' Thomas arched an enquiring brow and Oliver nodded. He owned a Mercedes, too, but the four-wheel-drive vehicle was obviously the safest choice tonight. It wasn't the weather for breaking the speed limit, and he was likely to run into some really nasty conditions after he crossed the Severn Bridge.

By the time he'd had his shower and dressed again, it was dark. The short winter afternoon had given way to a bitterly cold evening and he wasn't looking forward to the long journey into Wales. Downstairs, Thomas had the promised coffee, and some soup as well as a sandwich, waiting. 'Just to warm you up,' he said apologetically as Oliver came into the kitchen.

Thomas's own apartments were in the basement of the building. Oliver had his darkroom there, too, and on summer evenings Thomas sometimes served his meal in the sheltered charm of the walled garden at the back of the house. Tonight, however, the paved patio was a transparency in black and white, the reflection in the windows of the room behind giving the scene an eerie beauty.

The phone rang again as Oliver was drinking the soup, and this time Thomas had no hesitation about answering it. 'It's Miss Harlowe,' he said, covering the mouthpiece with his fingers. 'Do you want to speak to her, or shall I tell her you've already left?'

'And lie about it?' mocked Oliver drily. Then, taking pity on the old man, he held out his hand. 'I'll speak to her,' he said, deciding he owed Natalie an explanation of where he was likely to be for the next few days. 'Hi, sweetheart. It's good to hear your voice. Have you missed me?'

'Do you care?' Oliver stifled a sigh at the realisation that Natalie was angry with him, as well. 'I've been expecting you to call all afternoon. I rang the airport and they said your plane had been delayed, but—'

'I got back about half an hour ago,' Oliver interrupted her quickly. 'I was going to ring you, but—well, things came up.'

'What things?' Natalie was not placated.

'A phone call from my mother,' said Oliver, taking a bite from his sandwich. Then, chewing rapidly, he added, 'She's been trying to get in touch with me, too.'

'Are you eating?'

Natalie sounded outraged and Oliver swallowed before attempting to speak again. 'Yeah,' he said resignedly. 'I'm just trying to fortify myself for the journey. I've got to drive down to Penmadoc tonight.'

'Penmadoc!' Natalie gasped. 'You're not serious.'

'I'm afraid I am.' Oliver shook his head at Thomas when he mimed making him another sandwich. 'My stepfather had a heart attack two days ago.'

'Oh! Oh, I'm so sorry.' Natalie was all sympathy now. 'How is he? Is it serious?'

'He's dead,' answered Oliver flatly. 'That's why my mother wants me to drive down there tonight. I am her only blood relative. Naturally she wants my support.'

Or did she? Oliver wasn't absolutely sure what his mother wanted. She'd been decidedly strange when he'd spoken to her. Despite the years they'd spent together, he would never have expected Griff's death to affect her so badly.

'Would you like me to come with you?'

Natalie was speaking again, and for a moment Oliver was tempted. But then he remembered Laura and his refusal was automatic. 'I don't think so, sweetheart,' he said. 'Funerals are family occasions, as you know. And I'm not sure what the arrangements are yet.'

'Will your stepsister be there?'

Natalie's enquiry sounded innocent enough, but Oliver sensed her irritation. Ever since he'd mentioned the fact that his stepsister had brains as well as beauty, Natalie had resented her; which was ridiculous really when they'd never even met.

'She may be there,' he said now, evenly. 'But, if she is, I'll be the last person she wants to see.'

'Do you expect me to believe that?' Natalie snorted. 'I haven't forgotten what you told me about her flinging herself at you when she was hardly more than a kid!'

Oliver swore silently then scowled. He must have been drunk if he'd told Natalie about that. 'You didn't believe me, did you?' he scoffed, striving to sound incredulous. 'Come on, baby, I was only kidding. For God's sake, it's been over eight years since Laura and I even met!'

Natalie was silent for a moment, and then she said cautiously, 'So she didn't come to your room and get into bed with you?'

'No!' Oliver stifled a groan. He must have been drunker than he'd thought.

'And your mother didn't find out and threaten the pair of you?'

'I've said no, haven't I?' Oliver knew he could do without this. 'Come on, Natalie, I was only having a bit of fun. You're so gullible sometimes, I can't resist teasing you.'

'You bastard!' Natalie swore now. 'You were so convincing. I thought it was true.'

'So sue me,' he said, desperate to avoid any further revelations. 'Look, sweetheart, I've really got to get going.'

'But what about the Rices' party?' Fortunately, she was easily diverted. 'Couldn't you come back tomorrow? Surely there can't be that much you can do.'

'Except be there for Ma,' suggested Oliver drily. 'I'm sorry, baby, but you're going to have to go on your own.'

'Don't I always,' muttered Natalie, not altogether truthfully. 'Oh, all right. But you will ring me and let me know what's going on?'

'I promise.'

Oliver was relieved to escape so easily, but after he'd hung up the phone the images Natalie's words had evoked were not so effortlessly dispelled. This was not the time to be thinking about Laura, he thought impatiently, or to be remembering what had happened that unforgettable summer night. Or why, instead of taking up his place at university that autumn, he'd left the country, spending a year trekking around Europe, trying to get what had happened out of his system.

'You do realise it's after six, don't you, Mr Oliver?' Thomas's anxious tone interrupted him. 'I'm sure it's not wise to drive down to Wales tonight. There's reduced visibility on the M4 and the motoring organisations are warning people only to travel if it's absolutely necessary. Don't you think your mother would understand if you—?'

'Forget it.' Oliver pushed away from the table. 'As far as Ma's concerned, this is an emergency. Besides, there's always the chance that the weather could worsen. I don't want to find I can't get there tomorrow because they're snowed in.'

Thomas shrugged. 'Well, if you're determined...'

'I am.' Oliver was adamant. 'But don't worry, old man. I won't do anything rash. If I find I'm getting into difficulties, I'll find a motel.'

'You hope.'

Thomas wasn't convinced, and Oliver grimaced at the negative vibes he was giving off. 'Look, I've got to go,' he said.

'Don't you think I've got enough to contend with without you jumping all over me as well?'

Thomas sniffed. 'I'm only thinking of your welfare, Mr Oliver.'

'I know.' Oliver paused to give the old man a rueful look.

'But I must say, this is the first time I've seen you so determined to obey your mother,' he added peevishly, and Oliver's lean face creased into a mocking grin.

'That won't work either,' he said, looping the strap of his rucksack over his shoulder. 'Now, I'll phone you tomorrow, wherever I am, and I'll give Stella your condolences, shall I? I'm sure you don't want her to think you don't care.'

'I've already offered Mrs Williams my condolences,' retorted Thomas indignantly. 'Although I have to say she didn't seem to want any sympathy from me.' And then, because the affection he had for his employer was genuine, he said, 'Do take care, won't you?'

'I will.'

Oliver patted the old man's shoulder in passing, and then, after a regretful thought about the photographs he'd planned to process tomorrow, he picked up his keys and started for the door.

CHAPTER TWO

LAURA shivered.

Despite the heat that was still emanating from the old Aga in the corner, the kitchen at Penmadoc was decidedly chilly tonight. The cold struck up through the soles of her mules and she wondered why Stella hadn't had the stone floor removed and modern tiles installed in their stead. She could guess why, of course. The kitchen was still Aunt Nell's domain and even Stella baulked at locking horns with her. Besides, she doubted if Stella ever entered the kitchen except to issue orders. Domestic duties and cooking had never appealed to her stepmother.

But it was a relief to find that some things at Penmadoc hadn't changed when so much else had. Her father was dead. Impossible to believe, but it was true. Stella was the mistress of the house now. Laura was only here on sufferance.

Was it really only six months since she'd seen her father in London? He'd seemed as hale and hearty as ever, if a little more boisterous than usual. She'd put that down to his usual high spirits at seeing her again, but she wondered now if it had been a screen for something else. Stella had said that she'd known nothing about him having any heart trouble, but he could have been hiding it from her, as well.

Her stomach quivered. If only she'd known. If only she'd had some premonition that all was not as it should be. But although her grandmother had been a little fey, as they said around here, and had occasionally been able to see into the future, Laura never had. Whatever powers she'd possessed had not been passed on to her granddaughter.

According to her stepmother's version of events, her father's attack had been totally unexpected. He'd apparently

16

been out riding earlier in the day. Although he hadn't been a member of the local hunt, he'd always enjoyed following the hounds and, despite the fact that snow had been forecast, he'd ridden out that morning as usual.

Then, also according to Stella, he'd arrived home at three o'clock, or thereabouts, and gone straight to his study. She'd found him there a couple of hours later, she said, slumped across his desk, the glass of whisky he'd been imbibing still clutched in his hand.

Laura expelled a trembling breath. She hoped he hadn't suffered. When she'd spoken to her boss at the publishing house where she worked in New York, he'd said that it was the best way to go. For her father, perhaps, she thought now, but not for the people he'd left behind. Aunt Nell had been devastated. Like Laura herself, she could see the writing on the wall.

She shivered again as tears pricked behind her eyelids, and, dragging the folds of her ratty chenille dressing gown closer about her, she moved nearer to the hearth. Thank heavens they still used an open fire in winter, she thought, hunching her shoulders. There were still a few embers giving out a tenuous warmth.

She sighed and glanced about her. She'd come downstairs to get herself a glass of hot milk because she couldn't get to sleep. She was still on eastern standard time and, although it was after midnight here, it was still early evening in New York. She'd decided a warm drink might help, but the milk was taking so long to boil. Perhaps she should have looked for a hot-water bottle and filled that. At this rate, she'd be frozen before she got back to bed.

She started suddenly as an ember shifted in the hearth. At least, she thought it was an ember. There had definitely been a sound like something falling either in here or outside. She was feeling particularly edgy this evening and she was very aware of being alone downstairs. With the snow falling heavily outside, Penmadoc had an air of expectancy that was hard to ignore.

The milk came to the boil at the exact moment that some-one tried the outer door. The sound was unmistakable, the latch rattling as it had always done when the bolt was still in place. Laura's breath caught in her throat and she was hardly aware that the pan was boiling over until the hob started sizzling and the acrid smell of burnt milk filled the room.

'Oh, God,' she groaned, dragging the pan off the heat. But she was more concerned about who might be trying to get into the house at this time of night. As she listened, she was almost sure a masculine shoulder was applied to the door-frame, and while she stood there, frozen into immobility, an audible curse accompanied another assault on the latch.

Breathing shallowly, Laura left the smoking pan on the Aga and edged towards the long narrow lobby that opened off the kitchen. There was no door between the kitchen and the passage where boots and coats and other outdoor gear occupied a row of pegs. Stella called it the mudroom, but that was just an affectation. It was a lobby, plain and simple, that protected the kitchen from the immediate chill when you opened the outer door.

Breathing shallowly, Laura sneaked a look into the pas-sage. There was definitely someone outside: a man, judging by the muffled oaths she could hear even through the door. But human, she assured herself, despising her timidity. Pushing away from the archway into the kitchen, she stepped nervously into the passage.

'Who's there?' she called sharply, consoling herself with the thought that the door was apparently impregnable.

'Who the hell do you think it is?' the man snapped. 'Didn't you hear the Jeep?'

'The Jeep?' Laura frowned. She hadn't known anyone was expected tonight. 'Do you mind telling me who you are?'

'What?' His incredulity was audible. 'Open the door, Ma, and stop f—mucking about.'

Ma!

Laura's stomach clenched. Oh, no, it couldn't be. Not tonight, not when she was wearing this old dressing gown that she'd found at the back of the closet upstairs. She'd put it on for comfort, because her father had bought it when she was a teenager. But it wasn't particularly clean or flattering, and it clashed wildly with her hair.

'O—Oliver?' she ventured weakly, realising that she'd have to admit him, and he seemed to become aware that she wasn't his mother, after all.

'Laura?' he exclaimed. Then, evidently reorganising his reaction, he said, 'For God's sake, is that you, Laura?' She heard him blow out a breath. 'What are you doing? Waiting up for me?'

Laura fumbled with the bolts at the top and bottom of the door and then, turning the heavy key, she pulled it open. 'Hardly,' she said, keeping her eyes averted as she stepped back to let him in. 'Don't you have a key?'

'Don't tell anyone, but they've yet to invent a key that can open a bolt,' he retorted, and she guessed his sarcasm was an attempt to hide his own surprise at seeing her. He shook himself, dislodging snow from the shoulders of his leather jacket on to the floor of the passage. Then, sniffing expressively, he asked, 'What's that awful smell?'

'I burnt some milk,' said Laura defensively, closing and locking the door again before brushing past him into the kitchen. She knew she must look a sight with her hair mussed and her eyes still puffy from weeping. Not the image she'd wanted to present to the stepbrother who hadn't seen her since she married Conor. 'Did your mother know you were coming tonight?'

'I thought so.' Oliver followed her into the kitchen. Then he gestured towards the Aga. 'Oughtn't you to do something

about that before anyone starts to think you're trying to burn
the old place down?'

'Your mother, you mean?' she asked tersely, plunging the
saucepan into cold water before snatching up a dishcloth to
mop the stove. Anything to avoid looking at him, she
thought, though she was perfectly aware of how attractive he
was.

'Possibly,' he said now, and she wished she hadn't jumped
so childishly to her own defence. She had told herself that
if—*when*—she saw Oliver again she would behave as if the
past was another country. She had no wish to go there; no
wish to resurrect his memories of the naïve teenager she'd
been. He set down his canvas rucksack and draped a garment
bag over the back of the old rocking chair that stood on the
hearth. 'Anyway, I was sorry to hear about your father. It
must have been a terrible shock.'

'Yes. Yes, it was.'

Laura didn't look at him. She merely lifted her shoulders
before continuing to scrub the burnt-in stains off the hob.

'It was a shock for me, too,' he added softly. 'Your father
and I might not have always seen eye to eye about things,
but in recent years I like to think we grew to respect each
other's views.'

Laura stiffened her spine and forced herself to glance in
his direction. 'In recent years?' she echoed, as her eyes took
in the fact that he was broader. But it only served to give his
lean frame an added maturity without adding any fat to his
long bones. 'I didn't know you spent so much time at
Penmadoc.'

'I don't.' He sucked in a breath. 'But you were in the
States whereas I was available. He used to come up to
London occasionally and, less frequently, I'd come down
here.'

Laura tried not to feel any resentment. After all, it wasn't
as if her father hadn't wanted her to come home. But, after
her marriage to Conor broke up, it had seemed to her that

she was a failure. At that, as in everything else, she mused bitterly. And Stella would never have let her forget it.

'He didn't tell me,' she muttered now, turning back to her cleaning, but she was aware of Oliver crossing the room to open the fridge door.

'Why would he?' Oliver asked, peering inside. 'I doubt if he thought you'd be interested.' He heaved a sigh. 'Is there anything to eat around here?'

Laura permitted herself to view his broad shoulders. 'Didn't you have any dinner?' she asked, and he swung the fridge door shut again with an impatient snort.

'Dinner?' His amusement was bitter. 'What dinner?' He gave a grunt. 'I just got back from Singapore late this afternoon. Ma had apparently been ringing for hours, trying to get in touch with me. I only stopped long enough to take a shower before driving down.'

'Singapore?' Laura's curiosity was showing and she quickly changed what she had been about to say. 'Haven't you had anything to eat at all?'

'Soup. And a sandwich.' Oliver glanced into the fridge again. 'Don't people eat any meat these days?'

Laura hesitated. Then she said, 'I expect Aunt Nell has the freezer stocked. She always used to do a weekly shop at the supermarket in Rhosmawr.'

'So she did.' Oliver gave her a sideways glance. 'I guess I'll have to make do with another sandwich.' His mouth took on a humorous twist as he looked at what she was wearing. 'That new?'

Laura held up her head. 'Don't you recognise it?' she asked coldly, and had the dubious satisfaction of seeing a trace of colour enter his lean cheeks. The fact that her own face was red, too, offered little compensation, however. Once again, she'd betrayed what she was thinking and laid herself open to his contempt.

But instead of making some sarcastic comment Oliver merely closed the fridge again and leaned back against it, arms folded across his chest. 'Okay,' he said quietly. 'Let's start again, shall we?' His green eyes were narrowed and glinting with suppressed emotion. 'I don't want to argue with you, Laura. I know this can't be easy for you—'

'You flatter yourself!'

'I mean losing your father,' he interjected harshly. 'For God's sake, can't you think of anyone but yourself? I know you don't like me, Laura, but this is one occasion when I'd have thought you'd have put other people's feelings before your own.'

Laura trembled. 'It's late—'

'Yes, it is. But not too late, I hope!' he exclaimed impatiently. 'Look, like I said, let's try and come to some kind of compromise, shall we? For—well, for your aunt Nell's sake, if no one else?'

Laura dropped the dishcloth into the sink and tightened the belt of her robe. 'Very well,' she said, and heard his resigned intake of breath.

'Very well?' he mimicked drily. He cast his eyes towards the beamed ceiling. 'Oh, Laura, don't make it easy for me, will you?'

'I said—'

'I know what you said.' He straightened away from the door. 'Okay.' He held out his hand towards her. 'Friends?'

Laura moistened her dry lips. She didn't want to touch him. Dear God, she'd have done just about anything rather than put her hand into his. But that was stupid! Stupid! Did she want him to think she was afraid of him, that she hadn't got over that childish infatuation that had almost ruined her life?

'Friends,' she got out, almost gagging on the nausea that had risen into the back of her throat, and his strong brown fingers closed about her hand.

His fingers were cold but the impact Laura had was one of heat, a fiery heat that spread up her arm and into her breasts, making them tingle with an unwelcome awareness.

The warmth of his breath invaded the neckline of her robe and she felt as if she was enveloped by his scent and his masculinity. An image of how he'd looked, lying naked and unashamed on his bed, flashed briefly before her eyes, and she suppressed a groan. But it was all she could do to prevent herself from jerking her hand out of his firm grasp.

'Hey, you're shivering,' he said, and Laura had to bite her lip to silence the instinctive denial. 'I'm sorry. I didn't mean to upset you, you know.'

'You didn't.'

But her voice was high and strained and he seemed to sense it. With an odd expression playing about his mouth, he lifted his hand and stroked the backs of his fingers down her hot cheek, and this time she couldn't prevent her automatic response. With a strangled sound, she jerked back from him, bruising her hip against the corner of the scrubbed pine table that occupied the centre of the floor.

'Laura!'

His irritation was evident, but she suspected neither of them was prepared for his reaction. Instead of letting her go, he went after her, his hand closing on the nape of her neck now, his thumb forcing her face up to his.

'Is this what an unhappy marriage has done to you?' he demanded, and she realised incredulously that he thought she was reacting to some lingering torment from her relationship with Conor. That the panic she was barely controlling was something to do with her ex-husband.

As if!

'I—' She didn't know what to say. Her head was swimming with the emotions his hard fingers were arousing inside her, and blaming Conor for feelings he had never been able to inspire seemed a cruel deceit. But... 'Just let me go, Oliver,' she said weakly. 'I—I'm tired.'

'Yeah, I know.' His thumb was caressing her ear now and she thought how incredible it was that he thought *he* could give her any comfort. 'Poor Laura. Do you have any idea how young you look in that robe?'

Laura felt faint. 'Please,' she said unsteadily. 'Please, Oliver…'

'It's okay. I know.' But just when she thought he was about to release her he changed his mind and, instead of moving aside, he pulled her into his arms. 'You can rely on me, baby,' he said huskily, pressing her face into his throat so that Laura could scarcely breathe. 'I'm here for you. I just want you to know that.'

'What the hell do you think you're doing?'

For a moment, Laura wondered if it was she who'd spoken. It was what she should have said, she knew that, but although the hand that had been stroking her shoulder slid away she sensed Oliver was reacting to a stronger will than hers.

A suspicion that was reinforced when Stella Williams' shrill voice continued, 'For God's sake, Oliver, have you taken leave of your senses? She's not back in this house for five minutes before she's trying to cause trouble between us.'

Laura's jaw dropped. 'I hope you don't think that I—that I—was encouraging him—'

'So what are you doing down here at this time of night?' demanded her stepmother scornfully. She sniffed. 'And what's that awful smell?' Then, turning to her son without waiting for an answer, she said, 'I suppose you got her to let you in. Why didn't you come to the front door? I told you I'd wait up.'

'I did come to the front door,' retorted Oliver shortly, giving Laura a studied look in passing. 'I thought no one was up. There were no lights that I could see.'

Stella pursed her lips. 'I must have fallen asleep for a few moments,' she said peevishly. 'Goodness knows, I've had little enough sleep since Griff passed away.' Her eyes glittered as they turned towards her stepdaughter. 'Just because some people seem perfectly able to forget why they're here—'

'Forget it.' Oliver's voice was harsh as it broke into her provocative tirade. 'Laura couldn't sleep either. She came down to get herself a hot drink and I disturbed her. That's why the milk boiled over. It was my fault. That's what you can smell. Burnt milk. Nothing else.'

'If you say so.' Stella gave Laura a disparaging look. 'Don't you have anything else you could wear?'

Laura shook her head. She had no intention of getting into a discussion about her appearance with her stepmother. 'If you'll excuse me,' she said, not caring whether they did or otherwise, and, putting his mother between her and Oliver, she made for the door. 'I'm going back to bed.'

It was easier than she'd thought. Neither of them offered any objections as she slipped out into the hall. The smouldering embers in the hall grate lit up the door of her father's study, giving her a moment's pause. She was briefly tempted to go in there and try and calm her racing blood.

But the possibility that Stella might decide to show her son where her husband had been found deterred her. Instead, she hurried up the stairs and gained the sanctuary of her room with some relief. Leaning back against the panels, she wondered why she always let Oliver upset her. Whatever he said, whatever he did, he couldn't help getting under her skin.

Straightening, she crossed the floor to the square four-poster she'd occupied when she'd lived here. Although her belongings had been removed and Stella had had the room redecorated, it was still reassuringly familiar to her. But this might be the last time she'd use it, she thought, tears filling her eyes again. Once her father's funeral was over, she'd have no excuse for coming here.

Her reflection in the dressing-table mirror gave her a momentary shudder. For a second, the face that had stared back at her had been her mother's. But she knew that was just because they looked alike. Pale face, pale grey eyes, wild red

hair that rioted in an untidy mass about her shoulders. No
wonder Stella had looked at her so contemptuously.
Compared to her stepmother, she lacked any sophistication.

As for Oliver: well, she preferred not to think about him.
She wasn't at all deceived by his attempt at conciliation. She
didn't know what game he was playing, but she had no intention of making a fool of herself again.

She sighed now, loosening the belt of her dressing gown
and flopping back on to the bed. It was impossible to come
here without being assaulted by her memories. And, no matter how she might regret it now, Oliver had been an integral
part of her growing-up.

She caught back a tear. She might have hated her stepmother for taking her mother's place, but she had never hated
Oliver. At ten years of age to his thirteen, she'd been pa-
thetically eager to be his friend. She'd never had a brother
or a sister before and she'd hero-worshipped him. She'd followed him around like a blind disciple, willing to do anything
he asked of her, hanging on his every word.

She hadn't been alone. He was a popular boy, and at the
comprehensive in Rhosmawr that they'd both attended he'd
never been short of companions. For almost six years, she'd
deluded herself that the girls who came and went in his life
meant nothing to him. Her infatuation had been such that
she'd convinced herself he was only killing time until she
grew up.

Stella had guessed how she felt, of course. Her stepmother
had always had far more experience of life than Laura's father, and to begin with it had amused her that her stepdaughter should have fallen so completely for her son. Stella hadn't
done anything about it. Perhaps she'd thought she could leave
that to Oliver himself. But she'd got a rude awakening when
she'd discovered them together, and despite the fact that
Oliver had defended her she'd despised the girl from then
on.

Laura groaned now and rolled over on to her stomach,

trying to still the raw emotions that were churning inside her. That was all in the past, she told herself. She'd got over Oliver when she'd married Conor. And she'd grown up long before she took her vows. All right, so the marriage hadn't worked out; but these things happened. Conor had been too young to make the commitment; too willing to leave all responsibility to her.

It was coming back here, she thought abruptly. She hadn't spent any length of time at Penmadoc since she'd left to go to university over ten years ago. Like Oliver himself, she'd left home as soon as her schooldays were over—though he'd deferred continuing his education for a year to go backpacking across Europe instead.

Her lips twisted. It sometimes seemed as if fortune had always smiled on her stepbrother, and it was hard not to feel resentful when her own life had followed such a different course. Although being caught up in the conflict that had ensued after a country's escape from a non-democratic government might not have seemed fortunate at the time, the pictures Oliver had taken and sent back to a London newspaper had ensured him a job in journalism after he'd got his degree. Since then, he'd become famous for his skill in capturing photographic images. Recently, a book of stylised black and white pictures of Alaskan wildlife he'd taken had made the best-seller lists. He worked free-lance these days, accepting commissions as and when it suited him. He also gave lectures: Laura knew because she'd attended one anonymously in New York.

Which was so very different from her own experience, she acknowledged ruefully. After—after what had happened between her and Oliver, she'd found it very hard to trust a man again. Besides which, although she'd got her degree in English, she was no genius. The fact that she'd got a job in publishing was due more to Conor's father's introduction to his brother, who owned the company, than any skill on her part, she was sure.

Conor's parents had been good to her. They were Americans, like their son, and had sent him to England primarily to improve his social skills. He'd told Laura after their marriage that it was her independence and self-sufficiency that had drawn him to her. She'd never told him why she'd had to learn to depend only on herself.

Expelling a weary breath, she cast off the old dressing gown and crawled between the sheets. They were cold now, and she realised she should have filled a hot-water bottle, after all. So what's new? she thought. Her whole life seemed to have been a study in retrospection. With Oliver Kemp the fulcrum at its core.

CHAPTER THREE

OLIVER awakened with a thumping headache.

For a while he lay quite still, trying to work out where he was and how he came to be there. He couldn't understand why his room felt so cold. It didn't get this cold in Malaysia. And if he wasn't there why couldn't he hear the steady hum of the Knightsbridge traffic? Despite double-glazing, he was always aware of the heart of the city, beating away just yards from Mostyn Square.

Then he remembered. Remembered, too, why his head was pounding as if there were a pile driver in his skull. He was in Wales; at Penmadoc, not in London. And it was the fact that he'd consumed the best part of a bottle of Scotch before falling into bed in the early hours that accounted for his hang-over.

He groaned. He should have had more sense. But after seeing Laura again and learning why his mother had been so desperate to get in touch with him he'd needed something to fortify his strength.

The will...

Levering himself up on his elbows, he endeavoured to survey the room without feeling sick. But the bed swayed alarmingly, and although he swung his feet on to the floor he had to hold on to the mattress to keep his balance. Dammit, he was too old to be suffering this kind of nonsense. In future, he'd sustain himself with mineral water and nothing else.

Cursing whatever fate had decreed he should return to England at this particular moment in time, he got to his feet. Then, steadying himself on the chest of drawers beside his wardrobe, he shuffled across the room like an old man.

Despite a lengthy exploration, there were no painkillers in

the bathroom cabinet. The light in there was blinding. He hadn't thought to pull down the blind the night before and the brilliance of sun on snow was the equivalent of a knife being driven into his temple. It was the kind of light he usually only saw through a filter, but right now the idea of estimating aperture, shutter speeds and distance was quite beyond his capabilities.

'For God's sake,' he muttered, jerking on the cord, only to have the blind rattle up again at lightning speed. He swore again, grabbing the cord and repeating the procedure. 'This is just what I need.'

At least the water was hot and he stepped into the shower cubicle and ran the spray at a crippling pressure. He hadn't looked at his watch yet, but he guessed it must be after nine o'clock. He could have done with a cup of Thomas's strong black coffee. Instead, he would probably have to make do with the instant variety which was all Laura's aunt ever had.

Fifteen minutes later, dressed in black trousers and a chunky Aran sweater, workmanlike boots over thick socks keeping his feet warm, he left the room. His hair was still damp and he hadn't shaved, but he doubted anyone would notice. If his mother was still in the same state she'd been in the night before, his appearance was the least of his troubles. So long as she felt she could rely on his support in her conflict with Laura, she'd avoid doing anything to upset him.

Despite the intensive-heating programme his mother had inaugurated over the years, the corridors and hall at Penmadoc remained persistently chilly. Why Stella should want to stay here when she could buy herself a cosy apartment in Carmarthen or Llanelli, he couldn't imagine. He found it hard to believe that she was so attached to the old place. There had to be more to it than that.

The stairs creaked as he descended them, but at least the fire had been lighted in the hall below. Flames crackled up the blackened chimney, and the logs split and splintered in the massive grate. Years ago, he supposed, the hall would have been the focal point of the whole house. According to Griff, parts of Penmadoc dated from the sixteenth century, but so much had been added on to the original structure that its origins were hard to define.

He had paused to warm his hands at the fire when a dark-clad figure emerged from the direction of the kitchen. He saw it was Eleanor Tenby, Laura's aunt. Although he knew she could only be in her fifties, she looked years older, her straight hair almost completely white these days.

An angular woman, she had barely tolerated him as a teen-ager. But, because Laura had been fond of him, she'd treated him more kindly than she had his mother. Then, when the family had broken up, she'd blamed him for Laura's exile, only softening again in recent years when she'd seen how much Griff looked forward to his visits.

'So you're up at last,' she remarked without enthusiasm, proving that, as always, nothing went on at Penmadoc without her knowing about it. 'I offered to bring you up some breakfast, but your mother said to let you sleep. If you're hoping that I'll cook you something now, you're too late.'

'All I want is some coffee,' said Oliver flatly, the thought of grilled bacon and fried eggs turning his stomach. 'Anyway, how are you? This—' He spread his hands expressively. 'It must have been a great shock.'

'It was.' The woman's thin lips compressed into a fine line. 'And you'll not find any consolation in the bottom of a bottle. No one ever improved a situation with alcohol.'

Oliver might have disputed that on another occasion, but this morning he was inclined to agree with her. 'Believe me,' he said, 'I'm regretting it. And I am sorry you had no warning that Griff was ill.'

'Yes, well...' Laura's aunt sniffed deprecatingly, somewhat mollified by Oliver's words. 'You always had more sensitivity than anyone gave you credit for.' She paused. 'I expect you know that Laura's here.'

Oliver nodded, and then regretted the action. His head

thumped and he raised a hand to the back of his neck. 'Do you have any aspirin?' he asked, wincing. 'I've got to do something before my skull splits in two.'

'Come along into the kitchen,' said Aunt Nell tolerantly, and without waiting to see if he was following her she started back the way she'd come. 'What you need is something to eat,' she added, despite the refusal she'd made earlier. 'You'll feel altogether better with a bowl of my oatmeal inside you. You don't want to be poisoning your system by popping pills.'

Aspirin? Oliver grimaced. He'd hate to think what she'd say if she found out he'd been offered cocaine. Thankfully, he'd never been interested in what some people called 'social' substances, but these days they were increasingly hard to avoid.

The kitchen looked much different this morning than it had done the night before. As in the hall, a cheerful fire was burning in the grate and the scent of woodsmoke was not unappealing. There were other smells he was not so keen on, like the many species of herbs that grew in the pots on the windowsills and hung in dried bunches from the beamed ceiling. But there was the smell of freshly baked bread, too, and the crisp crackle of roasting meat from the oven.

Aunt Nell watched him take a seat at the table, and then busied herself pouring milk into a pan. The same pan that Laura had burnt the night before, thought Oliver ruefully. But clean now and sparkling like new.

The idea of drinking some of the thick creamy milk that was farmed locally made him shudder, and he wished he could just help himself to a cup of coffee instead. But there was no welcoming pot simmering on the hob, and he guessed he'd have to make some instant himself if he wanted it.

To distract himself, he glanced out of the window. As he'd noticed when he'd drawn his curtains upstairs, it had stopped snowing for the present and the sun was causing the icicles drooping from the eaves to drip. But it was a white world, only marred by the skeletal shapes of the trees. However, the evergreens that surrounded the vegetable garden outside looked like snowmen with their clinging mantle of snow.

'Have you spoken to Laura?'

Aunt Nell's question was unexpected. 'Don't you know?' he asked, with faint mockery. Then, because her lips had tightened reprovingly, and she was trying to help him, Oliver relented. 'Yeah. She was up last night when I got here.'

'Ah.' Aunt Nell had made a pot of tea and carried it to the table. 'I wondered why she didn't have a lot to say before she went out.'

'Went out?' Oliver glanced at his watch. 'What time did she go out?'

'She said she wanted some air,' replied Aunt Nell evenly. She set a cup and saucer and some milk beside the teapot. 'Go on. Help yourself. It'll do you more good than taking pills.'

Oliver could have argued. He knew where the coffee jar was kept. But his head was still thumping and he couldn't be bothered. There was caffeine in tea, wasn't there? he thought. For the time being, he'd make do with that.

The dish of oatmeal wasn't long in following the tea. Laura's aunt sugared it liberally before passing it over. 'There,' she said, as he put down his cup. 'Get that inside you. I always say that breakfast is the most important meal of the day.'

Oliver was sure he was going to be sick, but he forced himself to swallow several mouthfuls of the oatmeal. He'd eaten worse things in Malaysia, after all. People there ate rice at almost every meal.

'So where has she gone?' he asked at last, reluctantly aware that he was actually feeling much better.

'Into the village,' replied Aunt Nell, tidying the dresser. 'She didn't have a lot to say, as I said.' She turned to give him an appraising look. 'What happened last night? Did you and she have a row?'

'No.' Oliver was indignant.

'I thought your mother was supposed to be waiting up for you,' continued the woman. 'What was Laura doing down here?'

'She'd come down to get a drink,' said Oliver patiently, aware that he was falling back into the old patterns of defensiveness where Eleanor Tenby was concerned. 'Ma had fallen asleep, or so she said. That's why I came round the back.'

'And Laura let you in.'

'Yeah.'

'But I imagine your mother eventually turned up.'

'Yeah.' Oliver regarded her with a wry expression. 'But you know all this, don't you? Laura went to bed as soon as Stella appeared.'

'So she didn't discuss her father's death with you?'

'No.' Oliver was wary. 'What was there to discuss? I already knew how he died. Stella told me when I rang. He had a heart attack. It must have been appalling for her, finding his body. Had he been seeing a doctor, do you know? If he had, he should have warned her.'

'Griff hadn't been seeing the doctor,' replied Aunt Nell firmly. 'When Tenniel Evans came to examine him after—afterwards, he was as shocked as anyone else. Who knows why he died? He's not here to tell us. Perhaps he'd had a shock—or a fall from his horse. It may be that we'll never know.'

Nevertheless Oliver sensed that Laura's aunt had her own opinion. Not that she was likely to confide that opinion to him. But the very fact that she was asking questions was unsettling. For God's sake, surely this was one occasion when she could have given Stella some support.

'Do you know what's in the will?' he asked now, forcing himself to deal with facts, not fantasies, and Laura's aunt lifted her thin shoulders dismissively.

'It's nothing to do with me,' she said, turning away, which

wasn't an answer. But Oliver guessed it was the best he was going to get.

'So—were you here when it happened?' he probed, deciding that in spite of everything he deserved to know the details.

'No.' She glanced over her shoulder. 'I was away for the day visiting a friend in Cardiff. Griff had said he was going out with the hunt, and your mother had arranged to go shopping, or so she said. She told me she'd be eating out and not to bother preparing lunch before I left.' She licked her lips. 'But I did leave Griff a sandwich.' She grimaced. 'He never touched it.'

'I see.' Oliver's headache was definitely easing now and his brain had started functioning again. 'So she was alone in the house when she found him. Poor old Stella. God, she must have been frantic!'

'I dare say.'

Oliver frowned. There was something about the woman's tone that caught him on the raw. 'Do you doubt it?' he exclaimed. 'For God's sake, even you must feel some sympathy for her. There can't be any advantage in finding your husband dead!'

'Did I say there was?'

'No, but—' Oliver broke off abruptly. Then, in a calmer tone, he continued, 'Look, I know you've never liked her, but in these circumstances we've all got to make compromises.'

Aunt Nell shrugged. 'If you say so.' She paused. 'Did your mother tell you she was alone when she found—Griff's body?'

Oliver stared at her shoulder blades, turned to him again now and jutting painfully through the fine wool of the sweater she was wearing over her worsted skirt. Her question disconcerted him. Why did she want to know that?

'Of course she was alone,' he said tersely. 'You know that. You were in Cardiff, as you said earlier.'

'Perhaps you should ask her why it was two hours before she discovered his body,' Aunt Nell remarked, looking at him over her shoulder. 'If she was here, why didn't she hear him come in?'

'Perhaps she did.' Oliver blew out an irritated breath. 'Have you asked her?'

'It's nothing to do with me.'

'Of course it is.' Oliver was impatient and it showed.

'Not according to your mother,' replied the woman smoothly. 'Now, if you'll excuse me, I've got work to do.'

Olivia wanted to question her further. He was angry, and he wanted to know what she meant by making out there was some big secret about Griff's death. There wasn't, he assured himself. Men of Griff's age had heart attacks all the time, and without doing anything as strenuous as riding to hounds.

As Laura's aunt let herself out of the room, he moved to the windows to stare out unseeingly. As always, he never came off best in any encounter with Laura's aunt, and while he knew she wasn't a liar he suspected she'd do anything to cause trouble for his mother.

He scowled, pushing his hands into the waistline pockets of his trousers and forcing the sunlit garden into focus. It was a pretty scene, he thought, considering the frame of poplar trees whose bare branches formed a stark contrast to their surroundings. He would use a colour negative, he mused, to take advantage of the band of sunlight that was presently creating a rainbow of artistry in the thawing icicles. Some of his best work had been done spontaneously, and his fingers itched to capture it on film.

But then his gaze alighted on the line of footsteps that led to the gate and all thought of photographic composition vanished beneath a wave of frustration. Laura was out there somewhere. The footsteps led in only one direction, away from the house, and he wondered what she had thought of what had happened the night before. Was she aware that if his mother hadn't interrupted them he'd been in danger of resurrecting the offence that had driven them apart all those years ago?

Dammit, was he crazy, or what? He hadn't wanted Laura then and he didn't want her now. What had happened had been a reaction to circumstances, that was all, and he ought to be grateful to his mother for preventing him from making an even bigger fool of himself.

And he was. *He was!* But that didn't explain why he'd needed to anaesthetise himself with Scotch before he could get to sleep.

CHAPTER FOUR

LAURA stood in the shadow of a huge snow-covered cypress, warming her gloved hands beneath her arms. She'd been about to enter the garden when she'd seen Oliver standing at the kitchen window and she'd drawn back automatically, his dour expression warning her that he wasn't in the best of moods.

Her heart skipped a beat. Damn, why had he had to be here? All right, perhaps that was unreasonable. His stepfather was dead and naturally his mother wanted her own flesh and blood around her at this time, but if only *she* hadn't had to have anything to do with him.

She'd considered booking into a hotel in Rhosmawr, which was the nearest small town to Penmadoc, but she'd quickly discarded that idea. It wasn't fair to her father—or to Aunt Nell—to behave as if she wasn't the daughter of the house, and just because Penmadoc wasn't her home any more that did not give her an excuse to stay away.

She wondered if Oliver and her father had become closer in recent years. It was possible. There was no doubt that her father regretted her unwillingness to visit Penmadoc, and with the width of the Atlantic between them they'd seen each other much less than he would have liked.

For herself, she'd thought it had been easier for all of them when she went to live in the United States. It had certainly been easier for her—to begin with, at least. In New York, she'd been able to put the past behind her, and, if the wounds she'd thought healed had only been buried beneath a layer of self-deception, by the time she'd realised it, she was able to cope with the pain.

She sighed. She would have to go in soon. It was threatening to snow again and her feet were freezing. She wasn't used to living in the country in winter. Winter in New York was a much more civilised affair altogether. The paths were always cleared; shopping malls were always heated; and her apartment was always comfortably warm.

Unlike Penmadoc...

She took a deep breath. She shouldn't complain about the house really. There'd been years when she'd considered it the most beautiful house in the world. Not that it was beautiful, she conceded honestly. Built of dark Welsh stone, it sometimes had a rather dour appearance. But its pitched roof was peppered with half a dozen tall chimneys, and when she was a child she used to tell everyone that she was lucky because Santa Claus would have so many to choose from.

She shivered, stamping the snow from her boots and preparing to open the gate into the garden. It was no use putting it off any longer. She had to go in and face whatever was required of her. What could happen in a few days, after all? Her father was dead. His funeral was all she should be thinking of.

And then she felt the breath freeze in her throat. Oliver was still standing in the window but his face was fading. As she watched, paralysed by the realisation that she was hallucinating, Oliver's strong face gave way to older, softer features. Hardly breathing, she watched as her father's face came into focus. He was gazing out at the garden with much the same expression that Oliver had been wearing—a mixture of anger and frustration.

Panic gripped her. This couldn't be happening to her. She wasn't psychic. She'd never been psychic. Her mother, perhaps: her grandmother, definitely. But not her. Never her.

But there it was. Her father was dead. *Dead!* Yet there he stood, wearing the russet-coloured lambswool cardigan she had sent him for his last birthday. His hair was grey, greyer than she thought it had been last summer, but just as neatly trimmed as ever, his military moustache framing the uncompromising curve of his upper lip. There was a thread of hectic colour in his gaunt cheeks and deep pouches beneath his eyes, as if he wasn't sleeping too well. *Sleeping!* Laura stifled the hysterical sob that rose into her throat at the knowledge that her father was *dead*, dammit. You couldn't sleep any sounder than that.

She groaned aloud. Dear God, what was happening to her? This had to be some wild hallucination, brought on by the thoughts she'd been having as she walked back from the village. She'd been thinking about her father and somehow her subconscious had conjured him up. It wasn't as if there was any resemblance between Oliver and Griff Williams.

She blinked and, as if proving the point, magically her father's image had disappeared. Oliver stood there as he had before, a cream Aran sweater hugging his much broader shoulders, his tanned features tough and uncompromising, perhaps, but blessedly normal. With knees that felt decidedly weak now, she opened the gate and trudged into the garden. She wasn't going to think about what had happened, she told herself. It had been an aberration, that was all, brought on by her emotional state.

Oliver saw her immediately and a look of relief crossed his face. And, for once, she was glad to see him. After the experience she'd had, she'd have been glad to see anybody, she thought unsteadily. Even Oliver, she acknowledged. A man towards whom she ought to feel nothing but contempt.

He had the door open by the time she reached the house and she offered him a stiff smile of thanks as she stepped inside. 'I was beginning to get worried about you,' he said, attempting to help her off with her parka, but she shrugged his hand aside and finished the job herself.

'Why?' she asked offhandedly, sitting down on a wooden bench and removing her boots. Her hands were trembling and she prayed he wouldn't notice. She'd hate for him to think that she was afraid of him.

'Because it's going to snow again,' he replied, waiting

until she stood up and walked into the kitchen in her stock-inged feet. Following, he paused in the doorway, watching as she extended first one foot and then the other towards the heat of the fire. 'And you look very pale.'

'I'm cold,' said Laura shortly, aware that the cold she was feeling came from inside and not out. 'Mmm, that's much better.'

'Okay.' Oliver was evidently prepared to accept her ex-planation. His eyes drifted disturbingly over the thigh-length flannel shirt worn over a black tee shirt and ribbed black leggings. 'Did you manage to get any sleep?'

Laura tucked the sides of her hair behind her ears before answering him. 'I slept very well, actually,' she lied. Then, because it was expected, she asked, 'Did you?'

'No.'

He spoke flatly and, glancing his way, she wondered if that was true. There was a slight puffiness around his eyes, but he looked much as she remembered from the night be-fore. Narrow cheekbones angled above an unshaven jawline, and his thin mouth had a surprisingly sensual curve. He had never had conventionally handsome features; his face was too strong for that. But he was the most attractive man she had ever seen.

'Perhaps your conscience was troubling you,' she said without thinking, and immediately regretted it. The last thing she wanted was to dredge up the past again, and she added quickly, 'I mean, because you weren't here when your mother needed you.'

Oliver's eyes narrowed. 'What do you know about that?'

'About what?' Laura's eyes strayed compulsively towards the window. She was half afraid she'd see her father's image gazing in at her now and a shiver slid uneasily down her spine.

'About the afternoon your father died,' said Oliver shortly. And then, noticing her shiver, he added, 'You are cold. Would you like some coffee?'

Laura was tempted to refuse, but the idea of a hot drink was appealing. More appealing than the isolation of her room at this moment, and she nodded. 'Thanks.'

Oliver filled the kettle and plugged it in before taking a jar and two mugs from the cupboard above the counter. He placed the cups side by side and spooned some of the coffee into each. Then he turned, folding his arms and propping his hips against the unit. 'What did your aunt tell you about—well, about what happened?'

'Not a lot,' murmured Laura, feeling another shiver feather her skin. Glancing round, she saw the rocker beside the fire and curled her long legs beneath her as she settled on to its cushioned seat. 'What your mother told you, I expect.'

'Yeah.' But he didn't sound convinced. 'I thought you might know more about it, seeing that you've been here for a couple of days.'

'I only arrived the day before you did,' protested Laura, frowning. 'Besides, what's there to know? Daddy had a heart attack. Your mother found him.' She swallowed. 'End of story.'

Oliver waited until the kettle had boiled and poured hot water into the mugs before continuing, 'So you don't know what the old lady was talking about?'

Laura blinked. 'I don't know what *you're* talking about,' she said, accepting a mug from him, shaking her head when he offered milk. 'Mmm, this is good.'

Oliver resumed his position against the counter. 'Did your aunt tell you Stella was on her own when it happened?' he asked casually, and Laura stared at him, at last realising that there was more to this than random interest.

'I—yes. Yes, I think so.' She paused, cradling her mug between her hands. 'Why? What has she said to you? That there was someone else here?'

Oliver shook his head. 'You know Aunt Nell. She didn't actually *say* anything.'

'Then—'

'It was just an impression she gave.' He scowled. 'She implied it was odd that Griff had been dead for a couple of hours before Ma found him.'

Laura's eyes widened. 'Was he?'

Oliver pulled a face. 'Surely she told you that?'

'No.' Laura was thoughtful. 'At least, I don't think so. Anyway, why should it be important?'

Oliver shrugged, taking a drink of his coffee. 'No reason.'

But she didn't believe him. 'Do you think your mother was lying?'

'It wouldn't be the first time.' And then, seeing Laura's pained expression, he groaned. 'God, I don't know. Probably not.'

Leaving the stove, he dragged a chair from the table and, swinging it round, he straddled it across the hearth from where she was sitting. Resting one arm across the back, he regarded her consideringly. 'What's wrong?'

His change of topic was unexpected and Laura's eyes were drawn towards the window again before she could stop herself. But, thankfully, her reaction meant nothing to him, and after assuring herself that she had imagined what had happened earlier she shook her head. 'What could be wrong?' she countered, feeling her hair brushing against her shoulders. 'Daddy's dead. What do you think is wrong?'

Oliver sighed. 'Okay. Point taken. But you did look as if you'd seen a ghost when you came in. I wondered if anybody had said anything to upset you.'

'Who?'

Laura resented his perception, and it showed. But, dammit, she was doing her best not to reveal how she was really feeling and having him daunt her at every turn was disturbing to say the least. Despite her best efforts, she was irresistibly aware of the taut seam of his trousers visible between the spokes of the dining chair, and the bulge of his sex evident beneath the soft cloth. His thighs were spread, long-muscled and powerful, his booted feet only a few inches from the legs of her chair.

'I don't know. Someone from the village, perhaps,' he said now. 'So—how long is it since you saw your father?'

Laura moistened her lips. 'Um—about six months, I suppose. I came to London last year. There—there was a conference. Daddy came up to meet me.'

'Was he okay?'

'I thought so.' Laura shifted uncomfortably. 'Does it matter?'

'I guess not.' Oliver paused. 'I'm sure he was pleased to see you.'

'As your mother is always pleased to see you,' retorted Laura, responding to the implied criticism. 'Do you see much of her these days?'

'When I can. Or when she wants something,' commented Oliver drily. 'I've become much more popular since she's proved I'm good for a handout.'

Laura stiffened. 'Why didn't she ask Daddy if she needed money?'

'Oh—' Oliver obviously regretted his careless words. 'You know Ma. She's always short of funds.'

'If that's a dig—'

'It isn't.' Oliver seemed weary now. 'Come on, Laura. All I'm saying is that Stella's always been reckless with money. She's never had enough for her own needs. I should know.'

'Well, it's why she married Daddy, if that's what you mean,' Laura said shortly. 'At least she won't have that problem now.'

'Laura—'

'I mean it. Daddy was very conscientious about paying insurances, that sort of thing. And then there's this house...' Her stomach tightened at the thought of losing Penmadoc. 'She can sell it, if she chooses to do so.'

'I wouldn't bank on that,' said Oliver drily before taking a gulp of his coffee, and Laura wondered what he meant.

'Because she needs somewhere to live?' she probed, but Oliver seemed to think he had said enough on that score.

'Yeah,' he said, before reverting to her earlier topic. 'I wonder why she didn't hear your father come in?'

Laura's brows lifted. 'Do you think she was out?'

'She could have been, I suppose.' Oliver expelled an exasperated breath. 'But if so, why didn't she say so? After all, she'd told the old girl she was going shopping.'

'There you are.' Laura had no particular desire to dwell on the circumstances of her father's death. 'And don't call Aunt Nell "the old girl". She's not that much older than your mother.'

'True.' Oliver conceded the point. Then, with another change of pace, he asked, 'Have you spoken to your father's solicitors yet?'

'No.' Laura felt a twinge of unease. 'Have you?'

'How could I?' Oliver was gazing into the fire now. 'I only learned about—about what happened last night.'

'Hmm.' Laura knew a sudden surge of regret. 'It's a pity Daddy didn't realise your mother was at home when he got back. You never know, there might have been something she could have done.'

Oliver nodded. 'I thought that, too.'

'Or if anyone else had been around,' added Laura, still musing. 'What did your mother tell you last night?'

'Not a lot,' said Oliver briefly, and Laura guessed her stepmother's prime concern had been for herself. Was that why he'd asked if she'd spoken to her father's solicitors? Because Stella didn't want any obstacle to stand in the way of her getting probate?

'I didn't know she'd managed to get in touch with you,' Laura continued when he didn't elaborate. 'I know she phoned your house several times yesterday but that man you live with kept telling her that you weren't there.'

'Thomas is not my partner, he works for me,' stated Oliver, clearly irritated by her description. 'And, as I told you last night, I'd just got back from Singapore that afternoon.'

'Mmm.' Laura refused to be intimidated. 'Whatever. He certainly got under your mother's skin.' She paused, and then asked reluctantly, 'What were you doing in Singapore, anyway? Photographing the Prime Minister or some other dignitary?'

'As a matter of fact, I've been in Malaysia,' replied Oliver mildly. 'I'd been invited to join an expedition going into the Kasong Gorge. You've probably never heard of it, but it's virtually inaccessible except down this narrow defile. I went with a party of naturalists who wanted me to film some of the rare plants and flowers that are found there.'

'And I suppose it will give you enough material for another book,' commented Laura offhandedly, and Oliver gave her a wry smile.

'It sounds as if you're jealous,' he remarked, arousing her indignation. 'Hey, how about if I give Neill and O'Roarke first refusal when the manuscript's ready?'

'That's up to you,' replied Laura carelessly, her initial inclination to refuse tempered by the knowledge that Conor's uncle, who owned the company, would not approve of turning an obvious best-seller down. Besides, she'd never been jealous of Oliver's success, despite everything that had happened. She hadn't advertised the fact that he was her stepbrother, of course, but that had had nothing to do with his work.

'I'm glad you came,' he ventured softly, and Laura wished he'd continued baiting her then; it was easier to deal with. 'I did wonder if you would,' he added. 'The weather's been so atrocious, apparently. What did Ma say when she gave you the news?'

'She didn't,' said Laura swiftly. 'Give me—give me the news, I mean. It was Aunt Nell who phoned.' She refrained from mentioning the fact that she'd wondered if her aunt had called with or without her stepmother's endorsement. Judging from the greeting Stella had given her, she was still *persona non grata* in this house.

'I see.' Oliver's dark brows had drawn together, and she sensed he didn't like his mother's attitude towards her any more than she did. 'Well, you're here now, that's the main thing. Stella will have to get over it.'

'Get over what?'

Laura was confused, but with another of his lightning shifts of mood Oliver changed the subject again. 'You've filled out,' he said, his gaze on her mouth almost palpable in its intimacy. His eyes lowered to her rounded breasts and a kernel of heat ignited inside her. 'Yes, you've definitely changed since I last saw you.'

'If you mean I've put on weight, that's hardly a compliment,' said Laura tightly, using anger to hide the turmoil that was seething inside her. She wasn't sixteen now, she thought resentfully, or even twenty-one, as she'd been at her wedding, which was the last time he'd seen her. 'What gives you the right to make personal remarks?'

'It was supposed to be a compliment,' he protested. 'When you got married, you were as skinny as a rake.'

'Gee, thanks. That makes me feel a whole lot better.'

Oliver blew out a breath. 'I mean it.' His eyes drifted over her again and she had to steel herself not to glance down. But she was sure her peaking nipples were visible despite the serviceable bra she was wearing. 'You look—good,' he continued huskily. 'You're not my little sister any more.'

'I was never your little sister,' retorted Laura. And then, realising she was in danger of saying too much, she forced herself to rein in her emotions. 'Anyway, where's Aunt Nell? It's not like her to let anyone else use her kitchen.'

Oliver shrugged. 'Does it matter?' He pressed down on the bar and got up from the chair as he spoke. 'Tell me about you, about what you've been doing since you got your divorce. I still don't know what happened between you two.' He paused. 'Was there someone else?'

Laura drew back into the rocker, wrapping the folds of her shirt across her breasts. She was half afraid he was going to touch her as he had the night before, and she felt a treacherous moistness between her legs.

'I'm sure you're not interested in me,' she declared, aware that in spite of her efforts her voice was sharp. 'Any more than I'm interested in you and your girlfriends.'

'I don't have any girl*friends*,' responded Oliver, a little impatiently. 'I have one girlfriend. Her name is Natalie Harlowe. You may have heard of her. She's a model.'

'Surprise, surprise!'

Laura couldn't prevent herself from looking up at him, her eyes rolling expressively as she mocked his words. Oliver's face darkened with annoyance, and she quickly returned her attention to the dregs of coffee in her mug, but she was aware of him gazing down at her, and her stomach quivered with remembered pain.

'You'd like her,' he said, after a moment. 'If you got to know her, that is. Or are you so cynical after your own experiences with marriage that you can't face the fact that some couples do succeed?'

Laura's lips trembled. If he only knew, she thought bitterly. It wasn't her marital experiences that had made her cynical, no matter what he thought. She wanted to tell him then, wanted to wipe the smug expression off his face with what was real. But she couldn't. She had never told anyone. And he was the last person she'd confide in, anyway.

'I'm sorry,' she said now, but although she managed a careless glance in his direction there was little apology in her tone. She took a steadying breath. 'But the famous photographer and his model,' she added, trying to make light of it. 'Isn't it just the tiniest bit of a cliché?'

'I don't photograph models,' Oliver countered tightly, and to her relief he strode away to deposit his empty mug in the sink. Then, with his back to her, he continued flatly, 'You and I need to talk, Laura. I think you're still carrying far too much baggage from the past.'

How dared he?

Laura uncoiled her long legs from the chair and stared at his broad shoulders resentfully. Just like that, he thought he could dispose of their history in a few words. If he'd cared about her feelings at all, he'd never have said such a thing to her. What the hell was he implying? That he thought she'd messed up his life?

'I don't think we have anything to talk about,' she retorted, before she could prevent herself. It was all right telling herself she shouldn't stir up all those old feelings, but here, in this house, the past seemed unpleasantly close.

'There you are.' He swung round. 'You are harbouring some kind of grudge against me. For God's sake, Laura, don't you think I've suffered enough over the years?'

'*You've* suffered?' For a moment, for a long, shuddering moment, she was tempted to tell him. As he stood there, staring at her with those cold, accusing eyes, she desperately wanted to tear his shallow world apart. But then common sense—and a dogged sense of pride—came to her rescue, and, shaking her head bemusedly, she said, 'I—don't think anything either of us can say can change how we feel about the past.'

Oliver's shoulders sagged. 'I had hoped you'd have forgiven me. God knows, it's taken me years to forgive myself.'

Laura swallowed. 'I have forgiven you,' she asserted. 'I just don't want to talk about it.' She turned towards the door. 'And now I think I'll go and find Aunt Nell. There may be something I can do to help her.'

'To help her—but not to help me,' said Oliver roughly, coming after her. And, before she could guess his intention, his fingers closed about her arm. 'God, Laura,' he groaned, and she was almost sure he bent his head to inhale the fragrance of her hair. 'Don't do this to me. Last night you said we could be friends.'

Friends!

It was all she could do not to utter a stifled sob of hysteria at his words. The violence of his reaction had shaken what little self-control she had. 'Let me go, Oliver,' she managed unevenly. 'I think you've forgotten why we're here.'

'I've forgotten nothing,' he retorted, and now she was sure he was dangerously close to exposing her charade. His hand slid down her arm, his thumb finding the sensitive inner curve of her wrist. 'Damn you, Laura, it wasn't all my fault.'

CHAPTER FIVE

'SO WHEN is the funeral?'

Natalie was obviously trying to be understanding and Oliver wedged himself more comfortably against the headboard of his bed and switched his mobile phone to his other ear.

'Tuesday, I think,' he said, trying to respond with an equal warmth, but it was difficult to put that scene in the kitchen with Laura out of his mind. It was just as well her aunt had turned up as she had, he thought savagely. God alone knew what stupid stunt he might have pulled if her arrival hadn't interrupted them.

'Tuesday!' Natalie groaned. 'But that's almost the middle of next week.'

'Yeah, I know.' Oliver managed to infuse some sympathy into his voice. He was loath to tell her he didn't actually know what arrangements his mother had made yet. She hadn't got around to telling him.

'But didn't he die on Wednesday?'

'Yes.'

'Then isn't six days rather a long time to...?'

'I believe there had to be a post-mortem,' broke in Oliver reluctantly. 'And the weather's pretty lousy, too.'

'Mmm.' Natalie sighed. 'I suppose so.' She paused, and then added more optimistically, 'But they say a thaw is on the way.'

'Oh, good.'

Oliver knew his voice was lacking in enthusiasm and he was hardly surprised when she picked up on it. 'You don't care, do you?' she accused him indignantly. 'You know I'm leaving for Antigua next Thursday. I had hoped I might be able to persuade you to come with me, but now it sounds as if I'm not even going to see you before I go.'

'I didn't plan it this way, Nat.' But he did feel guilty. He'd forgotten all about the Antigua shoot. 'I'm sorry.'

'Are you?' She didn't sound convinced. There was a pregnant pause. 'I suppose *she's* there.'

'Who?' He knew exactly who she meant, but he needed a few moments to get his thoughts in order.

'You know who!' she exclaimed shortly. 'Laura.' She clicked her tongue. 'How long is she staying?'

Oliver could feel an unpleasant tightening in his stomach. 'Does it matter?' he asked with what he hoped was casual indifference.

'Of course it matters.' Natalie sighed. 'I'd like to meet her. If she's coming up to town when the funeral's over—'

'I neither know nor care what her plans are,' retorted Oliver, with rather less discretion. 'In any case, I doubt if she'll have time to come to London.'

'Why not?'

Why not indeed?

He gritted his teeth. 'Her father's just died, Nat. There'll be—things to do; matters to attend to. Not least, her father's affairs to put in order.'

'But won't your mother be doing that?' asked Natalie in surprise, and Oliver had to acknowledge that it was a reasonable question.

'She—may need some help,' he said, cringing at his own duplicity. 'Look, you know what solicitors are like. These things can be—complicated.'

'In other words, you don't want to ask her.'

'Ask her?' Oliver felt blank. 'Ask her what?'

'To come and stay with you,' replied Natalie impatiently. 'Honestly, Oliver, why couldn't you just come right out and say it? You don't like her, that's obvious. I'm beginning to wonder exactly what did happen all those years ago.'

Oliver stifled a groan. 'Nothing happened!' he exclaimed.

'For God's sake, Nat, stop making a drama out of this.' He took a deep breath. 'All right. If it'll please you, I'll ask her if she wants to come and stay for a few days before she goes back to the States. How about that?'

Natalie sniffed. 'You don't have to sound as if I'm forcing you to do it.'

'For Pete's sake—'

'All right.' She expelled a hurried breath. 'That would be nice. So—so long as you promise we'll have some time alone together after I get back.'

Oliver was tempted to say she couldn't have it both ways, but he had no desire to start another argument so he assured her that he had no plans for leaving town again in the immediate future. Then, desperate to end the conversation before he said something more incriminating, he added, 'I must go, baby. I want to let Thomas know what's going on and there are still arrangements to be made.'

'I know.' Thankfully, Natalie seemed to accept this. Then, just when he thought he was home free, she cried, 'Hey, I've got a marvellous idea. Why don't you invite your mother up to town as well as Laura? It would be a break for her, wouldn't it? It might help her to put the funeral behind her. And you know how much I've wanted to meet your family.'

Oliver's lips twisted. 'I'll—think about it,' he said tightly, aware that Natalie had no idea what she was suggesting. 'Bye, sweetheart. Speak to you soon.'

'See you do.' Natalie suppressed what sounded suspiciously like a sob. 'I love you.'

'Yeah. Me, too.'

Oliver gave the automatic response, but he felt a shameful sense of relief when the call was disconnected. God, he thought grimly, when had his life become so complicated? It didn't use to be. Before he'd left for Malaysia, everything had seemed so simple. He had a job doing something he loved; he owned a house that was the envy of many of his friends; and he was in love with a beautiful woman who, amazingly, loved him in return. He'd thought nothing could change that. Dammit, how wrong he'd been.

Yet, if he was honest with himself, he'd have to admit that nothing had changed. Not outwardly, at least. He still had his work; he still had his house; he still loved Natalie and she loved him. So why the hell was he feeling as if everything he had achieved, everything he'd believed in all these years, was suddenly on shifting sands?

Laura.

He scowled. He didn't have to look far to find the answer. It was the way she'd looked at him earlier that morning, the—what? Pity? Revulsion? Contempt?—in her expression that had cut the ground out from under him. She despised him, that much was obvious, and believing that they might be able to forget the past and start again was as futile as hoping that his mother might have had a change of heart.

But she couldn't put all the blame on to him, dammit. What had happened had been as much her fault as his. If he'd responded to what had proved to be an irresistible provocation, then so be it. But he hadn't initiated that provocation. She had. And the sooner she stopped condemning him for something that had been inevitable from the moment she opened his bedroom door—

His breath caught in his throat as someone knocked at his door. God, he thought, raking back his hair with a slightly unsteady hand. History couldn't be repeating itself. Could it? Did he want it to?

Angry at the sudden quickening of his pulse, he swung his legs to the floor and got to his feet just as his mother put her head round the door. 'You decent?' she asked, and without waiting for a reply she slipped furtively into the room.

Oliver regarded her with a jaundiced eye, aware that it would have been all the same if he'd been stark naked. As always, Stella put her own priorities first, and she offered no excuse for invading his privacy.

'I've been looking for you,' she said, closing the door with what he considered an unnecessary measure of caution. 'What are you doing up here?'

'Do I have to answer that?' Oliver regarded his mother's negligée-clad figure without emotion. He tossed the mobile phone on to the bedside table. 'I was making a call.'

'To Natalie?' For some reason, Stella had decided to endorse their relationship. Probably to ensure that he wouldn't be tempted to make a friend of Laura, decided Oliver cynically. 'You must bring her to meet me some time. She's a very beautiful young woman. As a matter of fact, she reminds me of myself when I was younger.'

'Really?' Oliver gave her a retiring look.

'Yes, really.' Stella huffed a little, and gathered the two sides of her negligée closer together. 'Brr, it's cold in here. I told Griff that these radiators weren't powerful enough. But he always insisted that he couldn't afford to change them.'

'Perhaps he couldn't,' murmured Oliver drily, walking across to the windows and gazing out at the amorphous shapes in the garden. 'This place must eat money.'

'Not that much.' Stella glided over to the bed, seating herself where he had been sitting to make his call. 'Mmm, that's better,' she said, drawing the quilt over her shoulders. 'So— what did Natalie have to say?'

Oliver turned, resting his hips on the ledge behind him. 'Don't pretend you're interested.' He lifted his shoulders in an indifferent gesture. 'Have you decided what you're going to do?'

'No, I haven't.' Stella was abrupt now. 'What time have I had to think about the future? I've been too busy trying to come to terms with the present.'

Oliver blew out a breath. 'So what do you want?'

'Oh, Oliver, don't be so callous. Can't I come and have a private word with my own son without him thinking I want something?'

Oliver's mouth compressed. 'Do you want me to answer that?'

Stella pursed her lips. 'You don't care, do you? I'm your mother and you don't care that I'm about to be thrown out of my home.'

'You don't know that,' replied Oliver flatly. 'You're only guessing what Laura might do.'

'Well, I don't need a crystal ball to see how she's going to react when she finds out,' retorted his mother harshly. 'You've got to help me, Oliver. I'm relying on you for your support.'

Oliver sighed. 'I'll do what I can, of course, but—'

'But what?' Stella was emotional now. 'Are you telling me you won't help me?'

'Of course not.' Oliver groaned. 'I just don't know how you think I can help.'

His mother dabbed her eyes with the corner of her sleeve. 'The will,' she said, as he'd known she would. 'Do you think it's legal?'

Oliver was resigned. 'I don't think that's in question, do you?'

'But I'm—I mean, I *was*—his wife. I thought when a husband died a wife automatically inherited his estate.'

'Only if he hasn't left a will,' amended Oliver flatly. 'And even then things aren't always cut and dried.'

Stella made a sound of distress. 'I didn't even know Griff had made a will,' she protested, shredding the tissue she'd taken from her sleeve between agitated fingers. 'He didn't tell me. Don't you think he should have?'

'Well, it would have been more charitable,' Oliver agreed. 'But, for reasons best known to himself, he decided to keep it from you. Perhaps he thought you wouldn't understand.'

'He got that right.' There was little compassion in Stella's voice at that moment. 'It was a rotten thing to do. Making that little bitch his heir!'

'This house was in Laura's family before her mother married Griff,' pointed out Oliver evenly. 'He probably thought he owed her the chance of deciding what happens to it.'

'But it's my home!'

'It was hers,' Oliver reminded her mildly. 'And Maggie Tenby's before that.'

'So you are on her side. You don't care what happens to me.'

'I'm not on anybody's side,' retorted Oliver, unmoved by his mother's ready tears. He knew Stella could produce tears at the drop of a hat. But he had to give her the benefit of the doubt. 'I just think you should try to be practical about this.'

'Practical!' His mother's voice was shrill now. 'When I'm going to be driven out of my home at any minute.'

Oliver blew out a weary breath. 'As I said before, you don't know that.'

'Don't I?' Stella snorted.

'Well, if you hadn't found the will, you wouldn't be worrying about it. Not yet, at any rate. If there's anything illegal about this, it's the fact that you opened an envelope that wasn't addressed to you. If you'd waited—'

'Until after the funeral, you mean?' His mother sneered. 'I suppose you think I should have let that prig, Marcus Venning, tell me that Griff had done the dirty on me. Oh, yes, he'd have enjoyed that.'

Oliver shook his head. 'You're exaggerating.' He paused. 'How did you find the will, anyway? Was it in Griff's desk?'

'As if.' Stella gave him a sulky look. 'Griff always kept anything of importance in the safe.'

'The safe!' Oliver stared at her aghast. 'I didn't know Griff had given you a key to the safe.'

'He didn't.' Stella shrugged. 'He kept it in his desk drawer.'

Oliver was appalled. 'You mean you riffled his desk before calling the ambulance services?'

'No.' Stella was defensive. 'I've known where it was for ages. I—just thought I ought to know. For—well, for emergencies.'

'Like his sudden death, you mean?' Oliver was scathing.

'Don't be horrid, darling.' Stella pursed her lips. 'I didn't know he was going to have a heart attack, for heaven's sake. He seemed perfectly all right when he left the house on Wednesday morning.'

'You saw him before he left?'

'Well—no.' She sighed at her son's expression. 'You know how early the hunt goes out and what with the weather threatening snow…' She sighed. 'I assume he left about half-past-eight.'

'So how do you know—?'

'How do I know he was all right? Nell said so, of course. She's always up at the crack of dawn.'

Oliver frowned. 'And he hadn't said anything about feeling ill? The night before, for instance?'

'No.' Stella pouted. 'Oh, you might as well know, Griff and I haven't shared a room for the last couple of years. You know what old men are like. They snore, and it was getting me down. I thought it would be easier for both of us if we had separate rooms.'

Oliver shook his head. 'Griff wasn't that ancient.'

'I know that, darling. But lots of couples have separate rooms these days. Besides, it suited Griff as well as me.'

'Did it?'

'What do you mean? You don't think that was why Griff decided to make his will?'

'I'm not sure.' As his mother told him the will had been made quite recently, it was always possible. 'You never know, he might have begun to wonder if you still cared for him.'

'Oliver! How can you say such a thing? I loved Griff.'

'I guess so.'

'You guess so?'

Stella was indignant now, but Oliver couldn't help recalling what she'd said when Griff had first asked her out. The fact that he'd owned Penmadoc and had a thriving veterinary practice besides in Rhosmawr must have dazzled Stella, who had been struggling, as a single mother, to support herself and her son. Stella didn't belong in Rhosmawr. Oliver had been born in London, but soon afterwards Stella had taken up with a Norwegian who had been working on the oil rigs, and followed him to Cardiff. Oliver had never known his own father, and his mother's relationship with the Norwegian hadn't lasted long. When Griff Williams had come on the scene, she'd been working as a waitress, and Oliver guessed she'd seen him as her last chance to make something of herself.

There hadn't been much talk of love in those days, Oliver remembered. He and his mother had been living in a poky one-bedroomed flat, and he'd had to make do with a shake-down on the couch. Which had been something of a handicap to Stella when she'd wanted to bring someone home. And there had been one or two boyfriends before Griff came on the scene, Oliver mused bitterly. Stella had been dangerously close to burn-out before the wealthy widower fell under her spell.

Chance was a strange thing, he acknowledged drily. If Stella hadn't offered to take old Mrs Weaver's cat to the vet, she'd probably never have met Griff. Or realised his potential, Oliver conceded. Stella had always been ambitious. She'd just never had the chance to do anything about it until then.

'Oh, Oliver, what am I going to do?' she groaned, distracting him from his thoughts. She slid off the bed and dropped the mangled tissue into the waste basket that stood just inside the adjoining bathroom door. 'You've got to help me.'

'I'll try.' Oliver sighed. 'But first of all you've got to promise me that you'll forget you ever saw the will.'

'How can I?'

'Just do it,' advised Oliver grimly. 'Remember, this is going to be a shock for Laura, too. And, as she's made a life for herself in New York, what makes you think she'll want to come back here to live?'

Stella's eyes widened. 'Do you think—?'

'I don't *think* anything,' said Oliver heavily. 'I'm just trying to make you see that it might be in your own best interests to behave as if you're in the dark. Laura isn't a monster.
She's hurting, too. And she may be prepared to be charitable.'

'Charitable!' It was obvious the word stuck in his mother's
throat. 'I don't want her charity. This is my house.'

'No, it's not,' said Oliver levelly. 'You might as well accept it. It isn't as if you're going to be destitute. You're going
to be very nicely provided for.'

'Forty thousand a year!' Stella was dismissive. 'How the
hell does he think I'm going to manage on forty thousand a
year?'

'Forty thousand a year is enough for anyone to live on,'
Oliver declared. 'Dammit, most people exist on a hell of a
lot less.' He paused. 'We did.'

'That was then; this is now. I'm not used to having to
scrape and save for every little thing I want. You know that,
Oliver. I thought you of all people would understand.'

'I do understand,' retorted Oliver sharply. 'I understand
that you've lived beyond your means for years.'

Stella caught her breath. 'I'll contest it. That's what I'll
do,' she declared, ignoring him. 'He won't get away with
this.'

'Ma!' Oliver was disgusted. 'You can't do that. You don't
have any grounds.'

'I know my rights.'

'No, you don't. A judge, magistrate, whatever, will probably consider you've been more than adequately provided
for.'

'With that pittance!'

'Do you know how much money Griff actually left?'

Stella held up her head. 'Not pounds and pence, no. But
there's this house, for one thing. It must be worth—I don't

know—half a million. And then he had insurances and things.'

Oliver sighed. He was tired of speculating about something his mother had no right to know about. Yet. 'Look,' he said, 'I suggest we leave it for the present. Until the will's been read—'

'But you'll be there for me, won't you?' Stella changed tack now, crossing the room, tucking her hand into his arm and resting her head against his shoulder. 'I don't know what I'd do if I didn't have you.'

Oliver tried not to reject her, but he could feel himself withdrawing, wanting to move away from her, to put some space between them even so. It had always been this way with his mother. She was perfectly willing to forget his existence for months on end, then something would happen, some imagined emergency, and she'd send for him, expecting him to behave as if they had a normal relationship when, in fact, they had never had that.

'Look,' he said. 'We can't do anything until after the funeral's over. Why don't you go and get dressed and then we'll discuss what arrangements still have to be made?'

'I can't think about things like that now,' protested his mother. 'Speak to Nell. She'll discuss things with you. She'll tell you what there's still to do.'

'I don't think so, Ma.'

'And don't call me that. You know I don't like it.'

Oliver shrugged. 'Whatever. I'll be in the study when you're ready to talk.'

'Not the study.'

Stella shivered, and Oliver realised he had spoken unthinkingly. 'The library, then,' he amended. And then, as she moved towards the door, he asked, 'Where were you when Griff had his attack, by the way?'

'Where was I?' Stella paused with her hand on the handle, gazing at him with wary eyes. 'What do you mean, where was I? You know where I was. I told you. I was here, of course.'

'In the house, yes. But actually where?'

She looked offended. 'Does it matter?'

'Humour me.'

She frowned. 'I was upstairs, if you must know. Lying down. I was—tired.'

'After your shopping trip?'

'What—? Oh, yes.' She swallowed quickly. 'Yes, after my shopping trip.'

'So you didn't hear him come in?'

'I—may have done.'

'But you didn't come down to see how he was, anything like that?'

'What is this? Some kind of inquisition?' Stella was angry now. 'Do you think I haven't tortured myself with the knowledge that if I had come down I might have been able to do something to help? It was terrible, Oliver! Terrible! I never want to go through anything like that again.'

Oliver hesitated. 'And—you were alone when you found his—I mean, him?'

'Of course I was alone. What else?' Her eyes narrowed. 'What has Nell Tenby been saying?'

'What could she say?'

Oliver turned the question back on her and with an exasperated toss of her head Stella jerked the door open. 'I suggest you apply that agile mind of yours to finding a solution to my situation instead of interrogating me about events that are immutable,' she declared coldly. 'Just remember where your loyalties should belong.'

The door slammed behind her and Oliver expelled a tired breath. That was all he needed: for his mother to think he had turned against her. Knowing how much Nell disliked his mother, could he really give any credence to anything she said?

Just the same...

He turned back to the window. The snow had stopped again, but the sky was heavy with the threat of more. He wondered if it would delay the burial, and then remembered that the Tenbys had their own vault in the churchyard here in the village. Griff would be laid to rest there beside his first wife. His worries were over, but Oliver had the unpleasant feeling that his own were just beginning.

CHAPTER SIX

MARCUS VENNING arrived on Monday morning.

Laura had spent the weekend trying to avoid both Oliver and his mother and she was surprised when Aunt Nell came to find her in the drawing room to tell her that the solicitor was waiting in the library.

'I thought you'd prefer to see him in there rather than in your father's study,' the older woman said gently, squeezing her shoulder. 'I think he wants to discuss the arrangements for after the funeral with you.'

Laura gave her a puzzled look. 'With me?' she said. 'Are you sure he doesn't want to speak to Stella?' After all, as her father's widow, she was his next of kin. And, as far as she knew, Oliver had spent most of the weekend dealing with the funeral arrangements. Surely he was better equipped to deal with the situation than she was.

'He wants to speak to you,' insisted Aunt Nell firmly. 'Are you up to it?'

'Oh—well, yes. I'm up to it.' Laura put the newspaper she had been scanning without interest aside and got to her feet. 'Where are the others?'

'She's still in her room,' declared Aunt Nell disparagingly, and Laura knew exactly who she meant. 'As for Oliver—I think he went out after breakfast.'

Laura was tempted to ask where he'd gone, but Oliver's actions were nothing to do with her. Apart from an occasional comment at meals, they hadn't spoken to one another since Saturday morning, and she told herself that that was how she liked it.

She followed Aunt Nell out of the room and then left her to cross the hall to the library. This used to be one of her favourite rooms, with its tall bookshelves and squashy arm-chairs, and she paused in the doorway, half expecting to see her father warming himself before the open fire.

But this thought was quickly suppressed. Thankfully, she had had no more hallucinatory experiences, and she'd managed to convince herself that she must have imagined the whole thing. Now the sight of Marcus Venning sitting at the table in the window, studying some documents he'd taken from his briefcase as he waited, restored her equilibrium, and she smiled as she walked towards him, holding out her hand.

'Mr Venning.'

'My dear.' Marcus Venning rose to his feet at her entrance and came to take her hand between both of his. 'I'm so sorry about your father. He was a good man. He'll be sadly missed.'

'Yes, he will.' Laura managed to blink back the tears that had flooded her eyes at this greeting. 'It's good to see you again, Mr Venning. It must be—eight years since we last saw one another.'

'And in much happier circumstances,' he agreed, releasing her hand to put both of his behind his back. 'Your wedding,' he added, as if she needed the reminder. 'Is your husband with you?'

'Um—no.' Laura indicated that he should resume his seat and took the chair opposite. 'Didn't Daddy tell you? Conor and I were divorced three years ago.'

'Oh...' He was clearly embarrassed. 'I'm sorry. I wouldn't have mentioned it if I'd known.'

'It doesn't matter. Really.' That was so true. She hated to admit it, but since seeing Oliver again she'd realised just how specious her marriage to Conor had been.

'Well, if you're sure...'

'I am.'

'Then I'm glad.' He grimaced. 'Not that you're divorced, of course. But that you've obviously found happiness with someone else.'

Laura coloured now. 'I—wouldn't say that.'

'Oh, but I thought—' He was evidently finding this confusing. 'Aren't you still living in New York?'

'Yes. But that's because my work is there,' she explained, glad that Oliver wasn't around to eavesdrop on this conversation. 'Er—how can I help you?'

'Ah…' The elderly solicitor shuffled the documents he had been looking at earlier into some semblance of order and stuffed them back into his briefcase. 'Well, now, I know this must be very painful for you, my dear, but I just want you to know that—that when the time comes you can rely on my support.'

'Thank you.'

Laura gave a small smile, and acknowledged that it was good of him to come all the way from Rhosmawr to tell her that. And in such conditions. Although the snow had stopped and the thaw had set in, the roads were still treacherous.

'You'll know, of course, that I had a phone call from your stepmother yesterday evening?' he went on after a moment, however, and Laura had to revise her opinion about his reasons for coming.

'I—no,' she admitted, realising she couldn't lie about it. She hesitated. 'Is there a problem?'

'Well, yes.' Venning sighed. 'If Mrs Williams is confined to her bed—'

'Confined to her bed?' Laura couldn't let that go unchallenged. 'I didn't know she was confined to her bed.' She tried to think. When had she last seen Stella downstairs? Saturday evening? Yes, that was it: Saturday evening.

'Well, according to Mrs Williams, the doctor is of the opinion that this has all been too much for her,' continued the solicitor ruefully. 'I fear she may not even be well enough to attend the funeral—'

'No!' Laura was incensed. 'No, that's not true.'

'Well, if your stepmother is prostrate with grief—'

'Prostrate with grief?' Laura hadn't noticed that Stella was prostrate with grief. On the contrary, she'd observed at dinner on Saturday evening that although the rest of them had only picked at their food Stella had eaten everything that was put before her.

'I know you've never been particularly fond of your step-mother, Laura,' the old man put in gently, and she felt a surge of indignation at the thought that so far as the solicitor was concerned it was she who was being unfeeling. 'But in the circumstances, my dear...'

'Stella isn't confined to her bed,' she insisted. 'Why would she say a thing like that?'

'Perhaps she's taken this harder than you think,' drawled an infuriatingly familiar voice, and, glancing over her shoulder, Laura found her stepbrother lounging in the open door-way. The bristle of his overnight beard darkened his jawline and he was apparently still wearing the clothes he'd worn to go out in. His booted feet were crossed and his parka-clad shoulder was propped indolently against the jamb.

'Oliver.' Marcus Venning evidently viewed this intrusion with some relief. 'How are you, my boy?' He got to his feet. 'I'm sorry we have to meet again at such an unhappy time.'

'Yeah.' As if finding his manners, Oliver straightened and came into the room to shake the old man's hand. 'It's good to see you, too, Marcus. You're looking well.'

'Thank you.' While Laura struggled to contain her indig-nation at the casual way Oliver had addressed the solicitor, Venning was visibly flattered by his comment. 'So I don't look as if I'm ready to be put out to grass yet?'

'Never.' Oliver grinned. 'I hope my—sister's been looking after you. As you've heard, Ma's indisposed right now.'

'Your sister—'

'I'm not his sister,' snapped Laura coldly. 'And at least now that Oliver's here he can confirm that his mother's—confinement—is purely voluntary.'

Oliver's dark features tightened. 'As I said before, I think Ma's finding it all very distressing.'

'Do you think I'm not?'

Laura was indignant, but Oliver ignored her outburst. He looked at Venning. 'You understand, don't you, Marcus?'

'What? Oh—I—well, of course.' Marcus nodded, but Laura resented the look that passed between the two men at that moment. It hinted at an accord she couldn't begin to share and she got up from her seat because she couldn't bear to sit still any longer.

'So—was there anything else?' asked Oliver, taking over the conversation, and she stared angrily at him. How dared he behave as if she was too stupid to handle the situation herself?

'Oh, yes.' Marcus looked up from the briefcase he had collected from the table. 'I did wonder if Laura might like to go and see her father before—before tomorrow.' He reached out to pat her hand. 'I'd be happy to accompany you, my dear.'

'If she'd like to go, I'll take her,' declared Oliver at once, earning a look of outrage from his stepsister. But Laura was still trying to come to terms with the fact that Venning had meant her father's *body*, which was lying in the Chapel of Rest at Rhosmawr, and couldn't immediately think of any valid reason why she might refuse his offer. 'I'm sure you've got other commitments, Marcus,' Oliver added, just in case she was tempted. 'There's no need for you to put yourself out when Laura's got family of her own.'

Laura's jaw dropped. The Kemps were not her family, she thought bitterly. But again Marcus Venning chose to accept her stepbrother's offer at face value.

'Well, if you're sure, Oliver,' he began. 'I must admit, I am rather snowed under at the moment, if you'll excuse the pun—'

'I'd prefer to go on my own,' Laura broke in, before he could go any further. She gave Oliver a contemptuous look. 'I'm sure you understand.'

'And how do you propose to get there and back?' he enquired, his pleasant tone masking the glitter in his eyes. 'You don't have a car.'

'Daddy does.'

'You're not planning on taking that old Daimler out in this weather—'

'Why not?'

'Look, there's no need for this.' Belatedly, Venning seemed to realise he had been a little premature in accepting Oliver's suggestion on her behalf. 'Laura can drive back to Rhosmawr with me.'

'And how will she get back again?' Oliver was frustratingly practical. 'It's okay, Marcus. We'll work this out.' He gave Laura a warning look. 'Somehow.'

Accompanying the old solicitor to the door, Laura found she was trembling. It wasn't so much a reaction to what had been said—though she did find Oliver's arrogance unbearable—as much as an increasing feeling of her own alienation here. This wasn't her father's house any more. The pictures, the furnishings, even the books that had been such an integral part of her childhood weren't hers to enjoy any longer. And the car, which she had so blithely said she'd borrow, wasn't hers to appropriate. Everything belonged to her stepmother now; and, by implication, to Oliver. No wonder he felt he could order her about. She was the outsider now, not him.

With the door closed behind the solicitor, Laura would have escaped to her room, but Oliver moved to the foot of the stairs to block her way.

'What are you going to do?'

Laura held up her head. 'That's my business.'

'Do you want to go and see your father?'

Laura's shoulders sagged. 'Look, don't push me, Oliver. I know you feel you have the upper hand here, but if I want to go and see my father I'll make my own arrangements, thank you.'

Oliver groaned. 'Why are you doing this? I've offered to

take you, and I will. But—' he sighed '—if you insist on going on your own, you can borrow my car.'

Laura attempted to move round him. 'No, thanks.'

'Why not?'

'I can get a taxi.'

'Yeah, right.' Oliver regarded her pityingly. 'Do you honestly think you're going to get a taxi driver to come all this way to pick you up, take you in to Rhosmawr and then bring you back again?'

'Why not?' she asked again, and he snorted.

'Get real, Laura. This isn't the States. Have you taken a look outside? The roads are treacherous. You may be lucky and persuade some sap to make the journey, but I wouldn't hold your breath.'

Laura shrugged. 'Then I won't go.'

Oliver swore. 'Can't you at least meet me halfway here? I don't offer the use of my car to just anyone. Take it in the spirit in which it's given.'

Laura hesitated. 'I don't know your car,' she admitted reluctantly. 'And, like you said, it is slippery out there. I'd hate to run it into a tree or something. I've seen your car. It's an expensive vehicle.'

'To hell with the car,' growled Oliver impatiently. 'I'd care more if you damaged yourself.'

Laura's lips twitched. 'Thanks.'

'So what are you going to do?'

Laura bit her lip. 'I suppose you'd better come with me,' she muttered, aware that she really didn't have a choice. She paused. 'If you've got nothing better to do.'

Oliver rolled his eyes. 'And if I do?'

'But you said—'

He shook his head. 'Get your coat,' he said resignedly, and she realised he had only been teasing her. 'I'll go and start the engine.'

Laura collected an ankle-length dark grey cashmere coat from her wardrobe to wear over the warm sweater and woollen trousers she'd put on that morning. Thick-soled Doc Martens ensured that her feet would remain dry and, gathering up her handbag, she hurried back downstairs.

Deciding she ought to let Aunt Nell know what she was doing, she went to the kitchen first. Her aunt was baking, and she looked up expectantly when Laura came into the room. Then, seeing that she was dressed to go out, she said, 'Where are you going?'

'I—er—I'm going into Rhosmawr with Oliver,' replied Laura a little awkwardly. 'Is that all right?'

Her aunt blinked, transferring a smear of flour to her cheek as she brushed a greying hair behind her ear. 'Has Marcus Venning gone?'

'Oh—oh, yes.' Laura had forgotten about the solicitor in her nervousness at going out with Oliver. 'He went a few minutes ago. Sorry.'

'So?' Her aunt looked at her. 'Are you going to tell me what he wanted?'

'Well, yes.' Laura frowned, trying to remember what the solicitor had said. 'He'd apparently had a call from Stella saying that she might not be well enough to attend the funeral—'

'What?'

'That's what I said.' Laura pulled a wry face. 'Apparently she told him that she's confined to her bed.'

'That's the first I've heard of it.'

'I said that, too.' Laura grimaced 'I think she let Mr Venning think Dr Evans had prescribed total rest.'

Nell said nothing to this. 'Is that the only reason he came?'

'No.' Laura licked her lips. 'I think he wanted to offer his condolences and—and to ask if I intended to go and see Daddy.'

'Ah.' The old woman nodded, and belatedly Laura realised that perhaps her aunt would like to come with them. 'So that's why Oliver is taking you to Rhosmawr.'

'Yes.' Laura hesitated. 'Would you like to come, too?'

'Why would I want to do that?' Nell shook her head. 'Wasn't I here when the poor man was taken away?'

Laura sucked in a breath. 'I never thought.'

'It doesn't matter.' Nell regarded her niece with concerned eyes. 'Are you going to be all right?'

'Why wouldn't I be?' Laura managed an upbeat response. 'Someone has to be. According to Oliver, his mother is finding it hard to come to terms with her loss.'

'Her loss!' Her aunt was scathing. 'That woman has never cared about anyone but herself.'

'Don't say that.' Laura didn't think she could stand any more unpleasantness. Not right now. 'I mean, it must have been awful for her, finding Daddy's—body and all.'

The older woman shrugged. 'If you say so.'

'Oh, Aunt Nell, I know you don't like her—nor do I—but we all have to pull together at a time like this. Don't we?'

'Sounds good to me,' said Oliver, coming into the kitchen as he spoke. 'Are you ready?'

CHAPTER SEVEN

THE sun was shining when they came out of the funeral home.

In Rhosmawr, the thaw was much more pronounced than in Penmadoc with only the occasional pile of slush at the side of the road to remind its residents of the previous week's storms.

Oliver had parked around the corner from the home and he sensed that Laura was glad to feel the warmth of the sun on her head as they walked back to the car. Seeing her father might have given her a sense of closure but he guessed that she wished she hadn't had to do it. The still, almost shrunken figure lying in the coffin had born little resemblance to the vibrant man she remembered, and he thought he saw her shiver as she climbed into the Jeep.

'You okay?'

He glanced her way as he got behind the wheel and Laura nodded. Despite the way she'd objected to his high-handedness earlier, he hoped she had been glad of his company during the ordeal.

'Fine,' she said at last, as if sensing that he was waiting for her to say something. 'Um—thanks for coming with me.'

Oliver's lips twisted. 'Yeah,' he said, not believing her but deciding it wasn't worth arguing over. He started the engine. 'Back to Penmadoc, right?'

'I mean it.' Before he could put the car into gear, Laura drew off her glove and touched his sleeve. 'I am glad I wasn't on my own.'

The impact of those slim fingers gripping his sleeve was electrifying. Although he was sure she wasn't aware of it, he felt as if a magnetic current was penetrating the thickness of the cloth. His pulse quickened; he could hear its clamour ringing in his head, and he stifled a groan of protest. For God's sake, what was happening to him? This was Laura, remember? Whatever immature emotions she had aroused in him were long gone, and the idea that he was having a sexual response now was not only unbelievable, it was insensitive and pathetic.

Something about his attitude, about the way he was staring at her, perhaps, caused Laura to withdraw her hand now, but the heat she'd generated inside him didn't subside. On the contrary, his palms were unpleasantly slick as they gripped the steering wheel and there was a definite feeling of fullness between his legs.

'Don't you believe me?' she asked, and a shudder of relief feathered his spine. At least she hadn't interpreted his behaviour the way he had, he thought with some relief. Her tongue appeared to moisten her lips. 'He looked very— peaceful, didn't he?'

'Yeah.'

Oliver dragged his eyes away from that pink tongue and thrust the Jeep into gear. Then, after checking that the road behind them was clear, he swung out to join the traffic. Thankfully, his actions were automatic and didn't require too much in the way of brainpower. Which was just as well, because his brain felt like mashed banana at that moment.

'I wondered…' She was obviously unaware of his turmoil and didn't even flinch when he went though a set of traffic lights as they were turning red. 'Why don't we have lunch on the way home?'

'Lunch?' His tongue clove to the roof of his mouth. 'Isn't your aunt expecting you back?'

'Maybe.' Laura regarded him out of the corners of her eyes. 'Is that your way of saying you don't want to have lunch with me?'

'It's not that.' Though God knew it was. Oliver took a calming breath. 'Okay. Why not? Where do you want to go?'

'I thought you might know somewhere,' she said quickly, lifting her shoulders. 'But perhaps it's not such a good idea. Your mother is bound to wonder where we are.'

Oliver had no desire to get into what his mother might think about him consorting with the enemy. Well, her enemy as she saw it, he conceded drily. 'Forget it,' he said, before he could change his mind. 'There's bound to be a hotel on the edge of town.'

'If you're sure.'

Her tone was much cooler now, and he sensed a rekindling of the hostility she'd shown towards him up till now. He guessed she was probably regretting making the offer. The feeling of sympathy they'd shared after leaving the funeral home was fast dissipating, and he cursed himself for allowing sex to govern his response. It was only lunch, dammit. Just because he'd become aroused when she'd laid her hand on him that was not her fault.

'I'm sure,' he said now, forcing himself to pay attention to their surroundings. 'Look, there's the Rhosmawr Moat House. Is that okay?'

Laura shrugged and he suspected she was having a hard time recovering her enthusiasm. 'If you like,' she said indifferently, and his mouth compressed. He'd asked for this, he thought irritably. It was his fault that she'd got totally the wrong impression.

They parked the car on the forecourt and picked their way around the pools of melting snow to the conservatory restaurant. Inside, the heat from more than a score of bodies had steamed the glass so it was impossible to see through the windows, but it was light and warm and friendly, and a pretty blonde waitress bustled over immediately to show them to a table in the corner.

'Can I get you anything to drink?' she asked, after they were seated, and Oliver arched an enquiring brow at his companion.

'Um—probably just orange juice,' she said, sliding her

arms out of her coat and draping it over the back of her chair. 'Thank you.'

'Orange juice?' Oliver sounded as exasperated as he felt. 'Wouldn't you prefer a glass of wine?'

'You're driving.'

'That's right. *I'm* driving,' he agreed, giving the waitress an apologetic look. 'You're not.'

Laura's cheeks had turned a little pink now. 'All right. A glass of white wine, then,' she said shortly, and he wanted to groan aloud.

'Fine,' he said instead, forcing a smile for the waitress. 'And I'll have a beer. The non-alcoholic kind. Thanks.'

Laura frowned as the girl walked away and, guessing what she was thinking, Oliver blew out a breath. 'I don't drink and drive,' he said, controlling his impatience with an effort.

Her shoulders gave a little bob. 'Oh—good. Nor do I.'

Oliver breathed heavily. 'So, is it okay?'

'It's nothing to do with me what you drink.'

'No, it's not. But that's not what I meant.' Oliver indicated the conservatory restaurant. 'Do you like this place?'

'It's okay.' Laura barely glanced around her. 'Do you come here a lot?'

'I've never been here before,' he said, shrugging out of his parka. Then he asked, suspiciously, 'Did you think I had?'

Laura toyed with her cutlery. 'I thought you must know the waitress,' she said offhandedly, and he caught back an oath.

'Why would you think that?'

'I don't know.' Although she wasn't looking at him, he could see she was uncomfortable now. 'She seemed very familiar.'

Oliver gasped. 'She was being friendly, that's all.'

'Mmm.' Laura didn't sound convinced. She picked up the laminated menu that stood on the middle of the table. 'Do we choose from this?'

'Why ask me?' Oliver was having a hard time hanging on to his temper. Then, because it wasn't really her fault, he said, 'Yeah. I guess so. Are you hungry?'

'Not very.' Laura scanned the menu without enthusiasm. 'I think I'll just have a tuna sandwich.'

'Right.' Oliver took the menu from her and made his own examination. 'I'll have a sandwich, too.' He breathed a little more easily. 'Here's our drinks.'

The waitress *was* very friendly, he noticed reluctantly. She smiled as she set down his beer and gazed at him with wide blue eyes when he gave their order. 'White or wholemeal?' she asked, after making a note of their selections. 'I suppose you're used to being offered loads of choices. When I was in Florida last year, I was amazed at how many different types of bread there were.'

'We're not Americans,' said Oliver, feeling obliged to answer her, and the girl gave Laura a questioning look.

'But I thought—'

'I've lived in the States for the past eight years but he's very definitely English,' explained Laura tolerantly, and Oliver intercepted the humorous look she cast in his direction. 'What part of Florida did you visit?'

'Oh, Orlando,' said the girl at once, including Laura in the exchange with evident reluctance. 'Disney World. Have you been there?'

'Yeah.' But Oliver didn't want to get into that. He gave a sardonic smile. 'Small world.'

'Isn't it?' she agreed, not getting the pun, and then, noticing that the manager was watching her, she added hurriedly, 'I'll get your order.'

She didn't hurry away, however. She sauntered, hips swaying provocatively towards the kitchens, and Oliver pulled a wry face when Laura arched her brows. 'All right,' he said. 'You were right and I was wrong. But, dammit, can I help it if women find me—?'

He broke off abruptly, belatedly aware of where his words

were taking him, and silently cursing himself for being so crass. As if she didn't already have a low enough opinion of him, he thought grimly, reaching for his beer.

But he saw Laura's eyes were twinkling as she looked at him across the rim of her own glass. 'Irresistible?' she suggested, finishing his sentence. 'Why, no, Mr Kemp, how could it be your fault? We ladies are just bowled over by your southern charm.'

Oliver grimaced. 'I'm sorry. I'm getting used to finding my foot in my mouth.'

'You're too modest.' Laura put down her glass. 'Anyway, I know you too well to be—surprised at your conceit.'

'Ouch.' But Oliver found himself grinning. 'Yeah, I guess you know me pretty well at that.'

'Which isn't to say that I approve of your attitude,' she appended swiftly. 'You always did have an inflated opinion of yourself.'

'Is that so?'

Oliver watched her with indulgent eyes. The tensions he'd felt towards her in the car seemed a million miles away now. Her mouth was curved, her lips had parted in a wide smile, and he realised suddenly how much he'd wanted her to smile at him.

Which was crazy really, remembering their history. Okay, they'd both been a lot younger then, a lot more naïve, he conceded, but those sorts of memories were dangerous now. God knew, he'd been attracted to her that summer she turned sixteen, but that was no excuse. Nor was the fact that it had been bloody hard for him to remember exactly how young she was.

His stomach tightened. He didn't want to think of that. What he'd done had been unforgivable, and she had every right to despise him for it. But, dammit, when she'd come to his room that night he'd been in no state to act sensibly. He should have sent her away. He knew that. If nothing else, the thought of how his mother would react if she found out should have deterred him. But it hadn't. Nothing like that had occurred to him. He'd been caught in the grip of an irresistible compulsion and his sex had governed his response.

In any case, Stella's reasons for resenting the relationship that was developing between her stepdaughter and her son had had little to do with their feelings. She'd been more concerned over what Griff might do if he discovered what was going on. And besides, she hadn't seen the way Laura looked at him, the way her eyes devoured him—or suffered the agony of stifling his arousal every time Laura came into the room.

Afterwards, she'd been furious, of course. And so eager that he should keep what had happened to himself. She didn't care about his morals, or the fact that he'd betrayed Griff's confidence. As far as she was concerned, Laura had started it. She'd deserved everything she'd got.

And because he'd been ashamed of his behaviour he'd let his mother persuade him not to talk about it. He'd taken her advice and kept out of Laura's way from then on. He'd consoled himself with the belief that Laura had regretted it as much as he had and would be grateful for his discretion, but he suspected now that it had been the worst thing he could have done. He'd let her think it had meant nothing to him. He'd let her believe that he didn't care how she felt. And then he'd compounded his guilt by clearing off to Europe, telling himself she'd forget all about him while he was away...

'What do you think your mother will do?'

Laura's voice aroused him from the pit of melancholy he'd made for himself, and he realised they'd been sitting for several minutes not saying anything. Her dark brows were lifted in mild enquiry and he felt a treacherous return of the emotions he'd felt before. Her grey eyes surveyed him, wide and gently appealing, shaded by dark lashes that showed a trace of red at their tips. Pale cheeks, only subtly tinged with col-

our, were a delicate foil for the wild beauty of her hair. It
tumbled about her shoulders, curling riotously, and although
it was the last thing he should have been thinking at that
moment an erotic image of himself burying his face in its
silky coils swept over him.

Oh, Lord, he thought, struggling desperately to remember
what she'd said. This was definitely not the time to be pic-
turing himself lying between her pale thighs, delighting in
her sweetness, revelling in her innocent sensuality, congrat-
ulating himself on arousing such an innocent response...

'Do?' he got out at last, struggling to interpret what she
meant. Had Marcus Venning given her any suspicion that the
will might not be as straightforward as she'd obviously expected? 'You mean, after the funeral?'

'Well, yes.' Laura frowned, white teeth nibbling at her
bottom lip. 'I assume she intends to stay at Penmadoc?'

Oliver took a deep breath. 'I think she'd like to,' he conceded weakly, and she nodded.

'Aunt Nell will be pleased,' she said. 'It's her home, too,
you see.'

Oliver hesitated. Evidently she didn't know anything about
the will. If she thought his mother would have allowed her
aunt to stay on at Penmadoc if she'd inherited the place,
though, she was very much mistaken. Despite her usefulness,
Eleanor Tenby had crossed his mother too many times for
her to expect any favours from her.

'It's your home, too,' he said now, resisting the urge to
stretch across the table and capture the hand that was lying
beside her glass.

'No.' Laura's expression hardened for a moment. 'No, it's
not. It hasn't been my home for over ten years.'

'Just because you don't live there any more doesn't mean
it's not your home,' replied Oliver evenly. 'I'm sure you
know they still call it the Tenby house in the village.'

'But we know it's not the Tenby house, don't we?' she

pointed out quietly. 'When your mother married my father, it became the Williams house instead.'

'I wouldn't be too sure of that,' said Oliver, before he could prevent himself, but happily the waitress returned at that moment with their food.

'One tuna and one bacon, lettuce and tomato,' she said, depositing the sandwiches with one hand and taking Oliver's empty glass with the other. 'Can I get you another beer?'

'Why not?'

Oliver wished he could have a lager. Right now, he would have preferred something stimulating instead of the non-alcoholic brew. His mother had put him in an impossible position, and he didn't like the thought that Laura was blaming her father for something he hadn't done.

'I'll have another glass of wine, too,' Laura said, before the waitress could move away, and just for a moment she and Oliver shared a teasing glance.

'Oh—right. The waitress took her glass, too, and then, evidently deciding she was fighting a losing battle, she added, 'I'll get your drinks. Enjoy your meal!'

In fact, neither of them was particularly hungry. Oliver watched as Laura picked at her sandwich, wishing there was something he could say to lighten her mood. It was obvious she believed that her father had left Penmadoc Hall to his mother, and that was why she was steeling herself for when the will was read.

'Tell me about New York,' he said, after their second round of drinks had been delivered and they were alone again. 'What do you do at this publishing house of yours?'

'Hardly mine,' she said wryly. 'As a matter of fact, it belongs to Conor's uncle. He gave me a job, you see, when Conor and I first moved to New York.'

'I see.' Oliver squashed a surprising twinge of jealousy. It was nothing to do with him if she chose to continue to work for the Neills. 'But isn't that awkward? You being his brother's ex-daughter-in-law, and all?'

'I thought it might be,' she conceded, sipping her wine in preference to the sandwich. 'But Jeff, that's Conor's father, was really nice about it.' She hesitated, and then said ruefully, 'I think he hoped we might change our minds.'

'About getting divorced?' Oliver knew that it really wasn't any of his business, but he couldn't deny he was curious about the man she'd chosen to marry.

'Mmm.' Laura seemed to realise who she was talking to and a guarded expression came into her eyes. 'But I'm sure you're not interested in me. My career has been singularly unimpressive when compared to yours.'

'I don't see what one has to do with the other,' said Oliver, frowning. 'And I am interested in what you've been doing for the past eight years. What you did after I left for Europe, for that matter. I did wonder if you might write to me. I sent Ma several poste restante addresses, but you obviously didn't want to know.'

Laura gave him an odd look. 'You are joking,' she said disbelievingly, and his frown deepened.

'No.' He paused. 'Why?'

'Oh, come on.' Laura gazed at him incredulously. 'Your mother was unlikely to have given your address to me.' Her face darkened suddenly. 'Besides which, I had nothing to say to you. You destroyed any faith I might have had in you when you ran away.'

'I didn't run away.' But Oliver could feel the heat in his cheeks and he wished they were not sitting in a public restaurant when the guilt he was feeling was on display. 'I'm sorry, but I thought it would make things easier for you,' he said defensively. 'It was going to be damn difficult going on as before.'

'For you.'

'For both of us,' he amended shortly. 'I was nearly nineteen, Laura. What the hell was I supposed to do?'

'What indeed?' She regarded him scathingly. 'I could say you were supposed to be going to Oxford in October, but obviously I was wrong. You wanted to get away, so you decided to delay your education. Backpacking in Europe must have been an inspiration. It enabled you to get away from me, from what I represented, as quickly as you could.'

'It wasn't like that,' he began, but she put up a hand to stop him.

'It doesn't matter any more,' she told him wearily. 'I don't care what your intentions were. As it turned out, you did us both a favour. You got the pictures that ultimately made you famous, and I learned to stand on my own two feet.'

Oliver stared at her impatiently. 'Why do I get the feeling that that's not the whole story?' he muttered harshly. 'For God's sake, Laura, I was hoping we could talk it out.'

'You're too late,' she said, draining her glass and setting it down on the table. 'If you're finished, I think I'd like to go.'

CHAPTER EIGHT

LAURA huddled into her chair beside the library fire. It was late, almost midnight, she thought, but she had little desire to go to bed. This might be the last night she'd spend at Penmadoc, and she wanted to make the most of it.

It was hard to believe that it was all over. Yet the funeral had been a dignified affair, in its own way. The priest who'd led the service had known Griff and that had come through in his eulogy, so that the words Oliver had spoken afterwards had had a poignant echo in what had gone before.

Despite their differences, Laura had been glad of Oliver's support throughout the service. Any sense of unreality had been banished by the presence of the flower-bedecked coffin, and she had found it hard to face the fact that she was now totally alone.

Stella had not attended.

Although Laura had been sure her stepmother would change her mind at the last minute and join the cortège before they left for the church, she hadn't. She'd continued to insist that she was at the mercy of her nerves, that she simply couldn't face the harrowing prospect of interring her husband, and that Griff would understand if he were here.

Actually, Laura rather thought he might. Her father had always been putty in Stella's hands. She'd known that, right from the beginning of their relationship, and although she'd tried to put her resentment aside Stella had never made it easy. She'd always been jealous of their relationship and it had been that, as much as anything, that had persuaded Laura to stay in New York after her divorce.

However, because Stella hadn't left her room all day, the will had not been opened. Which meant that although Laura had intended to leave for London the next morning her plans had had to be delayed. Marcus Venning had been most insistent that Laura should be present when her father's will was read, and despite her belief that her presence was only a formality she felt she owed it to her father to honour his last wishes.

His last wishes...

Her eyes burned. She had thought she was all cried out, but she had only to remember that she would never see her father again for the hot tears to dampen her cheeks. Poor Daddy, she thought, unable to deny her emotions. What a terrible thing it must have been to die alone.

The sound of the door opening behind her startled her. Scrubbing the heels of her hands across her eyes, she glanced across the firelit room. She had thought everyone else was asleep. Her aunt had retired earlier, worn out after greeting the many friends and acquaintances who had come back to the house after the interment to offer their condolences, and as Stella hadn't been available Aunt Nell had stood in her place.

But, to her astonishment, she saw it was Stella who appeared now. She came almost silently into the room, the folds of her dressing gown wrapped closely about her slim form. Laura had been sitting in the firelight, and with her legs coiled beneath her she was virtually invisible. Certainly, her stepmother didn't notice her as she glided across the floor.

Laura didn't know what to do. She didn't want to frighten the woman if she was suffering with her nerves, but at the same time she didn't want to remain unseen and later be accused of eavesdropping.

Goodness knew what Stella was thinking. Perhaps she'd come down to get a drink to settle the very nerves that had kept her from attending her husband's funeral. If so, should Laura speak to her? Was it possible that for once Stella might actually welcome her company?

But, before she could decide what to do, Stella had reached

the desk and picked up the phone. Her long, scarlet-tipped fingers punched out a number she obviously knew very well indeed, and then she put the receiver to her ear, tapping an impatient tattoo on the desk with her fingernail as she waited.

Laura shrank back into the chair. God, this was awful, she thought, stifling a groan. Unless she did something right now, she was going to be the unwilling recipient of her step-mother's confidence and that was the last thing she wanted. If only Stella had switched on the light...

It was too late. Even as it occurred to her that it was strange for Stella to be phoning anyone at this hour, her step-mother spoke. 'Jaz?' she said huskily. 'Jaz, is that you? Oh, thank God! I was afraid someone else might answer the phone.'

There was a pause then while whoever was at the other end of the line said something in their turn and then Stella spoke again. 'I know,' she said urgently. 'I haven't been able to do anything. The house has been full of people all day. I wanted to call you but I was afraid someone might listen in. That's why I'm ringing you from the library now. This way, I can be sure no one else is on the line. Yes, who else? Laura? No, I don't think so. She's far too full of herself to stoop to snooping on my calls.'

Laura could hardly prevent the gasp of indignation that rose into her throat. Who on earth was Stella talking to? Jaz? Who was Jaz? Male or female? And what right did they, whoever they were, have to suggest that she might do something so underhand? Even if...

Stella was still talking. 'No, I'm afraid not,' she murmured, and now there was a defensive note in her voice. 'I can't help that. I really wasn't up to dealing with it all today.'

Laura frowned. All what? What was she talking about? What could she possibly want to know? What could *Jaz* possibly want to know?

'I've no idea,' Stella persisted, suppressing Laura's spec-ulation. 'I mean it. I wasn't looking over his shoulder when he wrote it.' She broke off and then said fiercely in answer to whatever she'd heard, 'Well, yes. Yes, I expect so. What else can I do?'

The will. It had to be the will!

Laura smoothed her trembling palms over the knees of her woollen trousers, trying not to feel resentful of what was being said. After all, Stella had no idea she had an audience. It wasn't fair to judge her when she should have spoken up before her stepmother started the call.

When the door opened again, without warning, she didn't know who was the most surprised, herself or Stella. But when Oliver switched on the light and walked into the room there was no doubt that his mother's face showed her alarm.

'I've got to go,' she said, cutting the call short and slamming down the receiver. Then, gathering her composure, she turned to face her son with enviable restraint.

Laura really thought that Oliver had seen her. After all, the ceiling chandelier was casting light into all the shadowy corners of the room and her position seemed fatally exposed. But she'd counted without his very real irritation at finding his mother—his supposedly grief-stricken mother—recovered enough to come downstairs to make a phone call when she had a perfectly good connection upstairs. In consequence, his attention was focussed on her.

'What's going on?' he asked, his voice low and menacing, and Stella pushed her hands into the wide sleeves of her robe, as if to hide their reaction from him.

'I don't know what you mean,' she said. 'I should have thought it was perfectly obvious. I'm making a call, that's all. Is there anything wrong with that?'

Oliver's lips thinned. 'You tell me.'

'Tell you? Tell you what?' Stella was playing for time and Laura knew it. 'What can I tell you? I thought you were in bed.'

'Don't you mean *hoped*?' Oliver wasn't fooled for a moment, but with every passing second Stella was regaining her composure.

'Are you spying on me?' she demanded. 'How long have you been skulking about out there in the hall?'

'Not long.' Oliver regarded her steadily. 'Who were you phoning at this time of night?'

'That's my business.'

'Is it?' He pushed his hands into his trouser pockets. 'So why didn't you make the call upstairs?'

Stella heaved a sigh. 'My phone's crackly, if you must know.' Which wasn't true. 'Might I remind you that until the contents of the will are made public this is still my house? If I choose to phone a friend downstairs, so I don't disturb anybody, it's nothing to do with you.'

So it was the will she had been talking about on the phone. Laura frowned. But what did she mean, 'until the contents of the will are made public'? Surely she didn't suspect that Laura's father had left Penmadoc to someone else?

'I'd still like to know who it was you were calling,' Oliver persisted. 'For someone who only hours ago couldn't leave her bed, you've certainly made a swift recovery.'

Stella caught her breath. 'That's not true.' She pulled a tissue out of her sleeve and blew her nose noisily. 'It's a pity if you can't trust your own mother.'

'Yeah, isn't it?'

Oliver's dark eyes moved assessingly round the room and Laura wanted to curl up and die. Surely there was no way he could fail to notice her and she waited with baited breath for his denunciation.

But it didn't come and Stella was too eager now to escape further questioning to pay attention to anything else. Holding herself stiffly, she moved purposefully towards him. 'May I go now?'

Oliver shrugged without removing his hands from his pockets. He'd apparently shed the jacket of the charcoal suit he'd been wearing elsewhere and the darkness of his skin showed through the thin fabric of his white shirt. Laura was afraid he might not let his mother go until she'd answered his questions, but, as if deciding there was no point in pursuing it, he moved aside.

'Why not?' he said flatly. 'I can always press redial and find out who you were calling for myself.'

Stella's jaw dropped. 'You wouldn't do that!'

'Why? Is it a secret?'

Stella's face contorted. 'You're a beast, Oliver. I don't know why I put up with you.'

'You don't often,' he reminded her drily. Then, shaking his head, he said heavily, 'No, I won't do that.' But when her face lightened considerably he added, 'I'll find out some other way.'

'What other way?' Stella exclaimed warily, and Laura was again assailed with the fear that Oliver was about to expose her.

But all he said was, 'It will come out. These things usually do.' His lips twitched. 'You're not very good at keeping secrets, are you?'

Better than he thought, mused Laura bitterly, but Stella was speaking again.

'All right, all right,' she said, forcing a resigned tone. 'I was talking to Dilys, if you must know. You remember Dilys—Dilys James?'

'I know who Dilys is,' said Oliver, as Laura wished herself any place else but here. But *James*, she wondered tensely. Could that conceivably be the *Jaz* Stella had identified before?

'There you are, then,' Stella declared, brushing past her son. 'Now, if you'll excuse me, I'm going back to bed. I suggest you do the same.'

Oliver inclined his head, but he didn't answer her, and Laura guessed that, whoever she'd been phoning, Stella wouldn't risk making another call tonight. Not with Oliver on the prowl, she thought ruefully. Even Stella had her limitations. She just wished she knew how she was going to get out of the library without him seeing her.

The door closed behind her stepmother and then Oliver said softly, 'Okay. She's gone. Do you want to tell me what you're doing there?'

Laura's breath escaped on a shocked gasp as she uncoiled her legs. 'You—you knew I was here?'

'Not initially,' he admitted honestly, pulling his hands out of his pockets and raking them through his hair. 'I wouldn't have thought it was your scene.'

'My *scene*?'

'Eavesdropping,' said Oliver carelessly, and Laura swung her feet to the floor and stood up.

'You don't imagine I arranged—that?' she asked, flinging a hand towards the phone, and his brows quirked.

'You didn't?'

'No.' Laura was infuriated. 'I was just sitting here, quietly, minding my own business, when your mother came in.'

'In the dark?' he queried sardonically, and she gave him an indignant look.

'Yes, in the dark,' she agreed. 'I was thinking. I didn't know anyone else was up.'

'What were you thinking about?'

'I don't believe that's anything to do with you.' She paused, and then added unwillingly, 'I was reflecting about the funeral if you must know.' She straightened her shoulders. 'I wanted to thank you for your support today. I was grateful you were there.'

'Where else would I be?' Oliver's tone was rueful. 'He was my stepfather, you know.'

'He was your mother's husband, but she wasn't there,' pointed out Laura stiffly. And then, making to step past him, she said, 'I'm going to bed now.'

'Wait.' Oliver blocked her exit without effort. Then, as she gazed up at him with resentful eyes, he asked, 'Do you know who my mother was talking to?'

Laura stared at him. 'She told you.' She waited for him to acknowledge it and when he didn't she added shortly, 'Someone called Dilys, wasn't it? Dilys—James.'

'I know what she said,' said Oliver, scowling. 'I just wonder why she'd feel the need to ring a girlfriend at this time of night.'

Laura's lips parted. 'You don't believe her?'

'Let's say I'm open to suggestions.'

'Well, not from me.' Laura shook her head. She would have stepped past him then, but this time he put out a hand to stop her and she recoiled from the strength of his cool fingers on her wrist. 'Don't.'

'Don't what?'

His eyes were narrowed, but she was disturbed by the dark emotions glittering in their depths. 'Don't touch me,' she said, despising the panic in her voice. 'I can't help you.'

'Perhaps you can; perhaps you can't.' His thumb moved over the sensitive veins that throbbed with the pressure of the blood that was surging through them. 'You're not afraid of me, are you, Laura?'

'Afraid of you?' A squeak of outrage escaped her. 'We're not talking about me, remember?'

'Oh, yeah, I remember,' he told her huskily. 'I remember everything. Like you, I wish I didn't.'

'I think you're giving me too much credit,' she got out nervously, fighting the urge to tear her arm out of his grasp. 'As a matter of fact, I think coming here, meeting you again, has done me some good.' She swallowed a little convulsively. 'It's helped me to get things into perspective. Do you know what I mean?'

'I know what you're saying,' he said huskily. 'But perhaps I don't believe it.' His mouth quirked. 'Do you know what I mean?'

Laura winced. He was making fun of her. Having got no joy out of his mother, he'd turned his attention on her instead and she was a fool to let him get away with it.

'Why aren't you in bed?' she asked, desperately trying to maintain her composure in spite of his provocation. 'Have you—have you been out?'

'Out?' His tone was softly jeering. 'Oh, right. And where would I go?'

'You could have gone down to the village,' she retorted defensively. 'The pub's still there. You used to be quite a regular. And if you were bored—'

'Bored?' He moved closer and it was an effort to simply stand her ground. 'Who said I was bored?'

'You must be if you're reduced to tormenting me,' she replied tartly. 'What's the matter? Are you missing—what was her name?—Natalie?'

Oliver's mouth took on a palm-moistening sensuality. 'If I didn't know better, I'd wonder if there wasn't just a grain of jealousy in those words.'

'But you do know better, right?' exclaimed Laura flatly. 'My God, I sometimes wonder what I ever saw in you.'

It wasn't what she'd intended to say, but his arrogance had caught her on the raw and she was alarmed when he narrowed the space between them. 'Do you want me to remind you?' he asked, his breath fanning her cheek, and she smelt the faint aroma of malt whisky on his breath.

'No!'

He'd been drinking, she realised dully. That was what all this was about. He'd been drinking and, anticipating that she'd be leaving in the morning, he'd decided to amuse himself at her expense.

'Are you sure?'

'I'm sure.' She brought her other hand up to try and prise his fingers from her wrist, catching her breath when he captured that hand as well. 'I think you'd better let me go.'

'And if I don't?'

'I could call for help. I'm sure your mother would be only too eager to come to my rescue.'

'Yeah.' His lips twisted. 'Yeah, I guess she might, at that.'

'And you don't want to fall out with her, do you?' Laura persisted, not sure why she was provoking him. 'Particularly now.'

'Particularly now?' he echoed, and she steeled herself to meet his puzzled eyes.

'Now that she's going to be a wealthy woman at last,' she retorted maliciously, and saw the look of shock that crossed his face.

It had been an unforgivable thing to say and totally unjustified. As far as she knew, Oliver had never profited from his mother's marriage. Oh, he'd gained in small ways, of course. He'd always had plenty to eat, clothes to wear, a decent place to sleep, but any success he'd had he'd achieved through his own efforts and she knew it.

'I—I didn't mean that the way it came out,' she mumbled as he continued to stare at her, but instead of releasing her his fingers slid possessively up her arms.

'Which way did you mean it?' he demanded harshly. 'You as good as accuse me of only being here so that I can benefit from—what would you call it?—my mother's good fortune, perhaps, and I'm supposed to believe you didn't mean it?'

'No—'

'It sounded that way to me.' His lips twisted. 'It's good to know you've got such a great opinion of me. And as you have...' he jerked her towards him '...I might as well take advantage of the fact.'

Her breasts were crushed against his chest. The strong muscles of his thighs pressed against her legs. She wanted to resist him but the memories his hard body evoked were taking over, and she was left with only words to resist his appeal.

'Don't do this,' she pleaded as his hand cupped her nape, turning her face up to his. But resentment, anger—*frustration*?—was driving him on, and she was no match for his grim determination.

His mouth was hard at first, angry, almost bruising in the

way it forced her lips to part to allow the hungry passage of his tongue. It was not the way he'd kissed her all those years ago, but he'd had less experience then, and he hadn't wanted to hurt her as he did now.

Yet, for all that, she could feel his resentment weakening. He'd bound her hands behind her back with one of his, but now, as he sensed her unwilling response, he let them go. His hands shaped the yielding curve of her spine instead, before sliding over her buttocks, pausing to caress the sensitive cleft that was tangible through her clothes. Those caressing fingers tormented her, turning her bones to water, while a feverish heat swept up her thighs to pool wetly between her legs.

He must know how she was feeling, she thought unsteadily as he brought her fully against him. That was why he was letting her know how aroused he was. Despite his anger, he couldn't hide his body's reactions either and his shaft pressed intimately against her stomach.

Laura's body was burning. She'd forgotten what it was like to feel such an abandonment of self. Despite a couple of abortive affairs and a marriage that had been more of a business partnership than a love match, she'd had very little sexual experience. Only with Oliver had she ever lost control of her emotions, and although her head was spinning she knew she mustn't let it happen again.

Yet it was hard, so hard, to hang on to her reason. His mouth was gentler now, softer, his tongue caressing her lips, playing with her tongue, drawing the tip into his mouth and suckling greedily on it. His hand moved from her nape to the waistband of her trousers, lifting the hem of her sweater and exposing her bare skin. His hand spread on her midriff, his palm hot and slick against her ribs.

Laura's stomach plunged. Her heart was racing wildly, trying to restrain the mad rush of blood that filled her veins without success. Every muscle, every sinew in her body was alert to the sensuous brush of his thumb on the underside of her breast, and she had to steel herself not to rub her pelvis against his. But she wanted to; how she wanted to! And although she knew she was playing with fire she couldn't prevent her hands from sliding up his chest and tangling in the damp hair at the back of his neck.

He shuddered then, releasing her mouth to slide his lips along her jawline. 'God help me,' he muttered, pressing hot, hungry kisses against the curve of her throat, and it was the raw anguish in his voice that brought Laura to her senses.

'God won't help you now,' she taunted, somehow injecting a note of mockery into her tone. 'You'd better let me go, Oliver, before we both do something we'll regret.'

'Who says I'll regret it?' he demanded thickly, his strong fingers cupping her breast now, his thumb probing the taut nipple. 'This doesn't feel as if you object.'

'Appearances can be deceptive,' said Laura in a strangled voice. 'As—as you should know very well.' She swallowed on a convulsive sob. 'How about—how about—Natalie? Don't you think you owe any loyalty to her?'

Oliver scowled. 'Don't bring Natalie into this.'

'I didn't.' Laura's voice hardened. 'You did. Or are you as indifferent to her feelings as you were to mine?'

Oliver's fingers dug into her waist for a moment, but to her relief—or so she told herself—she could feel him withdrawing from her, physically as well as mentally. 'Why do you care how Natalie feels?'

'I don't.' To her shame, Laura knew that was true. 'But I hoped it was a way to stifle your libido. Nothing else seems to do it. Not even the fact that I don't want you to touch me. Not now. Not ever.'

And, because he let her, she was able to push him away and walk out of the room with just a semblance of dignity. But it had been a close call. On her part just as much as on his.

CHAPTER NINE

OLIVER slept badly; again. It was getting to be par for the course, he thought bitterly. And the headache he had when he awoke couldn't be blamed on the amount of alcohol he'd drunk either. He'd had a couple of drinks, sure, but he felt he'd deserved them after the day he'd had. And two drinks were not enough to account for the feeling of depression he had when he opened his eyes.

Of course, he wasn't denying that he hadn't expected to have a run-in with either his mother or Laura again the night before. He'd gone for a walk to try and clear his head and it had been pure chance that he'd been crossing the hall when he'd heard his mother's voice. What had she been doing, sneaking about the house making phone calls she could just as easily have made in her room? Had she really been phoning a girlfriend? Somehow, that explanation didn't ring true.

But had Laura believed it? That was what he'd like to know. She'd been in the room the whole time and had obviously heard more of the call than him. Would she tell him if she suspected his mother was lying? After what had happened after Stella had gone to bed, he somehow doubted it. What in God's name had possessed him to kiss her? She was never going to trust him again.

He scowled down at the plate of scrambled eggs Laura's aunt had provided for him. It shouldn't matter what she thought, but it did. Dammit, she'd practically accused him of taking advantage of her father and then imagined that pretending she hadn't meant it would pacify him. The trouble was, the knowledge of the will Stella had found was taking its toll on his nerves, and he'd been so mad that Laura should even *think* such a thing without any evidence, it had shattered

The Harlequin Reader Service® — Here's how it works:

Accepting your 2 free books and gift places you under no obligation to buy anything. You may keep the books and gift and return the shipping statement marked "cancel." If you do not cancel, about a month later we'll send you 6 additional novels and bill you just $3.34 each in the U.S., or $3.74 each in Canada, plus 25¢ shipping & handling per book and applicable taxes if any.* That's the complete price and — compared to cover prices of $3.99 each in the U.S. and $4.50 each in Canada — it's quite a bargain! You may cancel at any time, but if you choose to continue, every month we'll send you 6 more books, which you may either purchase at the discount price or return to us and cancel your subscription.

*Terms and prices subject to change without notice. Sales tax applicable in N.Y. Canadian residents will be charged applicable provincial taxes and GST.

If offer card is missing write to: Harlequin Reader Service, 3010 Walden Ave., P.O. Box 1867, Buffalo NY 14240-1867

BUSINESS REPLY MAIL
FIRST-CLASS MAIL   PERMIT NO. 717   BUFFALO, NY

POSTAGE WILL BE PAID BY ADDRESSEE

HARLEQUIN READER SERVICE
3010 WALDEN AVE
PO BOX 1867
BUFFALO NY 14240-9952

NO POSTAGE
NECESSARY
IF MAILED
IN THE
UNITED STATES

his self-control. He'd wanted to punish her, and that was what he'd intended. But when he'd taken her in his arms it hadn't worked out at all the way he'd planned.

To begin with, he'd been angry, but that hadn't lasted long. He'd been in control, too, but somehow that had got away from him as well. All his preconceived ideas had taken a beating, but not as much of a beating as he had taken himself.

He expelled an unsteady breath. Imprisoning her hands behind her back had seemed such a good idea, he remembered ruefully. It had made her helpless, vulnerable, susceptible to his every demand. It had also brought her upper body against his, stilling her resistance, but the sensual pressure of her breasts against his chest had aroused an entirely different reaction, after all.

Of course he'd expected her to resist him. He'd wanted her to, if only to prove he had the upper hand. But after those first few moments she'd been as caught up in their lovemaking as he was, and when her lips had parted beneath his he'd been lost.

He'd forgotten how delicious her mouth tasted. Soft, and hot, and so responsive—his blood had pounded like thunder through his veins. His arousal had been instantaneous; there'd been no way he could control that. He'd only buried his tongue inside her, but he'd wanted—how he'd wanted—to do so much more.

He'd let her hands go then, but instead of backing off the way any sane man would have done he'd allowed himself to explore her softness instead. He hadn't been able to resist the urge to bring her fully against him, and there'd been a pleasurable kind of pain in letting her feel his throbbing need.

He felt an unwelcome tightening in his groin at the memory. If she hadn't brought him to his senses then, it would have been too late. In his own mind, he had already stripped her trousers and sweater from her, and he was already imagining how sweet it would be to part those slick petals between her legs...

'Are you going to eat those eggs?'

Aunt Nell's down-to-earth tone caused an immediate reaction. He felt like a schoolboy who'd been caught looking at girlie magazines under the sheets. A faint colour invaded his tanned face, which he hoped she'd put down to the heat of the dining-room fire. He'd hate to think she could detect what was going on in his mind.

'I'm not very hungry,' he said, pushing his plate aside. Which was true. 'Thanks, anyway.'

The woman pulled a disapproving face. 'You need food,' she said. 'I've noticed that your appetite has been sadly lacking all the time you've been here. I can't believe that Griff's death is responsible, and I wouldn't have thought a man like yourself would have any trouble with his weight.'

Oliver gave her a wry look. 'Is that a compliment?'

'It's nothing but the truth,' averred Laura's aunt firmly. She paused. 'Now, do you know if your mother is planning on getting up this morning? Marcus Venning said he'd be back by ten o'clock and it's almost that now.'

'Is it?' Oliver was surprised. He'd spent longer than he'd thought deliberating over the eggs. 'As far as I know, Stella is planning on meeting Marcus this morning.' He forced a casual tone. 'Is Laura up?'

'Laura's been up for hours,' replied Aunt Nell, starting to clear the table. 'She had breakfast in the kitchen with me at seven o'clock.'

'So where is she?' Oliver's voice was sharp, but he couldn't help it. He was half afraid that now that her father was buried she'd decided there was no reason for her to stay.

'How should I know?' Aunt Nell didn't take kindly to being spoken to in that fashion. 'She went out about an hour ago. I didn't ask her where she was going.'

Oliver sighed. 'But you know, don't you?' he said, pushing back his chair and getting up from the table. His mouth compressed. 'Must I remind you that Marcus will want to see her, too?'

Laura's aunt gathered the remaining cutlery on to the tray and then looked up at him defiantly. 'I believe she's gone to the church,' she said. 'She said something about visiting her father before she left.'

'Oh...' Oliver breathed a little more easily. 'Oh, right. So she'll be back soon?'

'Very likely,' said the old woman, heading for the door. 'Oh, and by the way, Beth will be starting on the bedrooms directly. I asked her not to come in yesterday, what with the funeral and all.'

Oliver nodded. Beth Llewellyn came up several times a week from the village. Although Aunt Nell enjoyed running the house herself, she drew the line at doing all the heavy work. In consequence, Beth had been a part of the establishment since before his mother had married Laura's father, and although Stella complained that she was a gossip she wasn't prepared to participate in the housework herself.

Aunt Nell had gone back to the kitchen with the tray and, leaving the dining room, Oliver decided to go and check on the fire in the library. Marcus wouldn't be too happy if the room was chilly. Despite the old man's sprightly appearance Oliver knew he was troubled with arthritis in cold weather.

He also hoped it might serve to exorcise his memories of the night before. In spite of a determined effort to do so, he couldn't get the thought of Laura out of his head. Sitting at the square leather-topped desk, gazing out at the bare trees that were appearing again in the garden as the snow melted, visions of the past engulfed him. He found himself wondering when it was that he'd first noticed that Laura was growing up...

He guessed he must have been about seventeen when he'd realised she wasn't a kid any more. Not that he'd been attracted to her in those days. She'd been more of a nuisance than anything else, always wanting to know where he was going, and with whom; fouling up his relationships, cramping his style.

He'd seemed to spend his days trying to get rid of her, although he'd done his best not to hurt her even then. He'd been aware of the fragility of her confidence. Unlike his mother, he'd never believed that Laura was the brat she claimed.

He supposed he'd been lucky that the summer she turned fifteen, he'd taken a holiday job in Snowdonia. He'd worked at a café near the mountain railway and had spent his free time mixing with hikers and climbers from all parts of the world. That was when he'd first conceived his interest in backpacking, which had proved so advantageous the following year.

He'd begun taking photographs, too. Of his friends, to begin with, and then subsequently of the magnificent scenery in the National Park. Learning how to process the pictures himself had come later, as had the realisation that this was what he wanted to do with his life.

It was during his final year at Rhosmawr Comprehensive that his relationship with his stepsister had altered. At sixteen, Laura had had all the charm and freshness of a young woman, with the added bonus of not knowing exactly how attractive she was. Because she was taller than her peers, she'd walked with a certain diffidence, but Oliver had been fascinated by her slim limbs and long, long legs.

Her hair, of course, had been instantly noticeable. It had been longer then, a riot of fiery curls that fell almost to her waist. She'd said she hated it because people called her a redhead, but even in those days Oliver had known it wasn't red. It was actually strawberry blonde.

In any event, he'd found himself waiting for her, instead of the other way about, sitting with her at lunch break, walking her to the bus. Because her birthday was towards the end of the school year, in June, and his was at the start of the year, in October, there were only two school years between them, and pupils in the fifth year often mixed with pupils in the sixth year, so there was no one to object.

Not at school, at least.

At home, it was very different. His mother objected strongly to the attention he was paying to Laura. She'd warned him that Laura's father would never stand for it, though in all honesty Griff had never voiced any disapproval. On the contrary, he'd seemed pleased that his daughter and his stepfamily seemed finally to have settled their differences. He'd had no idea that his wife was as opposed to his daughter as ever.

The summer before Oliver was due to go to Oxford at the start of the Michaelmas term had been an unseasonably hot one. For weeks the temperature had hovered somewhere in the middle eighties, and he and Laura had spent much of their time trying to keep cool. The River Madoc that meandered through the village widened into a pool near Penmadoc Bridge, and it was a popular meeting spot for all the young people in the village. It was deep enough to swim, and the water was deliciously cold on a hot day.

They'd talked a lot that summer, about anything and everything, sharing their deepest thoughts and dearest wishes. Their relationship hadn't been like the relationships he'd had with other girls his own age. He'd been attracted to her, sure, but it had been her personality that had intrigued him. He'd wanted to be with her, but he hadn't had anything sexual in mind.

Or so he'd told himself.

He scowled now. It had been so easy to delude himself. So easy to pretend that the reason he liked looking at her was because she appealed to the artist in his soul. Her creamy skin, the freckles in her complexion, the provocative upthrust of her small breasts had given a natural sensuality to the photographs he'd taken of her, and he'd fooled himself that his interest was objective, or at least innocent of any prurient intent.

How Laura herself had interpreted his attentions was another story. Or perhaps it was the same one, only he'd been too blind to see where things were heading. During those long summer days, she'd become his soulmate, and he liked to tell himself he'd been unaware of how dangerous her attachment to him had become.

Until the night she'd come uninvited to his room...

The sound of a car's engine interrupted his thoughts. Marcus, he guessed grimly, half relieved at the sudden reprieve. God knew, he didn't want to think about what had happened between him and Laura at this moment. What had nearly happened the night before was still too blatantly vivid in his mind.

The door was pushed open a few moments later and Aunt Nell appeared. 'The solicitor's here,' she said, without ceremony, and stood aside to let Marcus Venning into the room. 'Will I tell your mother or will you?'

'There's no need for anybody to tell me anything,' retorted Stella's sharp voice behind her. 'I'm here.' She flashed her son a defiant look before turning to the solicitor and giving him a thin smile. 'Marcus,' she added, rather less belligerently. 'Punctual as ever, I see.'

The old solicitor huffed a little self-importantly. 'Yes, well, I always like to keep to a schedule,' he said, approaching the desk that Oliver had just vacated. 'I'm glad to see you're feeling much better this morning, Mrs Williams. It was such a pity you couldn't join us yesterday.'

Stella's lip curled. 'I wouldn't call it a pity that I couldn't attend my own husband's funeral. You don't imagine I wanted to let him down—'

'You were devastated, I'm sure,' remarked Venning drily, and Oliver suspected the old man was no more convinced of his mother's incapacity the previous day than he was. He deposited his briefcase on the desk and looked around. 'Where's Laura?'

'She's coming,' said Aunt Nell from the doorway. 'She's just taking off her boots.' She glanced behind her. 'She went to the church earlier.'

'Ah.'

Marcus accepted this explanation with an approving nod and Oliver saw the look of irritation that crossed his mother's face at the realisation that so far as the old solicitor was concerned Laura was still the mistress here. And always would be, he reflected, whether she chose to live here or not.

Laura's appearance a few moments later brought its own tension into the room. Oliver wondered if he was the only one who felt it or whether his mother was as indifferent to Laura's presence as she appeared. Surely she must feel some sympathy for her, he thought uneasily. At a time like this, they should have been able to support one another.

But, as usual, Stella chose to ignore her stepdaughter, and although Laura glanced a little uncertainly at her father's widow she didn't attempt to bridge the gulf that Stella had created between them.

For himself, Oliver had the greatest difficulty in keeping his eyes off Laura. She was wearing a skirt this morning, a pale heathery tweed whose hem ended a good four inches above her knee. He guessed it wasn't deliberate, but it exposed a considerable length of shapely thigh, particularly when she sat down and crossed her legs, and that, along with the vivid glory of her hair, was a potent combination.

'Good morning,' she said, her cheeks flushed from the cold air outdoors. 'I'm sorry if I've kept you waiting. I was talking to Father Lewis and I'm afraid I forgot the time.'

'I'm sure we all understand how that could happen,' Venning assured her warmly, earning another resentful look from Oliver's mother. He looked towards the doorway, where Aunt Nell was still hovering, half in and half out of the room. 'Come and sit down, Miss Tenby. You're a beneficiary, too.'

Laura's aunt looked as if she would have preferred to forego the privilege, but she was obliged to come into the room and take a seat. Then, after assuring himself that Oliver was quite content to remain standing in front of the fire, Venning seated himself at the desk and opened his briefcase.

There was no mistaking the tensions in the room now. Glancing at his mother, Oliver saw the way her knuckles were whitening over the arms of her chair. Even Aunt Nell couldn't hide her own uneasiness, and Oliver wondered if she was anticipating her departure if, as she expected, Griff had left the bulk of his estate to his wife.

If only she knew...

His lips twisted as the old man drew out an envelope. Marcus was enjoying this, he thought. He must know what was in the will and he was deliberately taking his time to prolong the suspense. Or perhaps he didn't know. Perhaps, like Laura and her aunt, he'd been kept in the dark. Perhaps he assumed Griff had left everything of importance to Stella. Maybe this was just his way of showing his disapproval, of dragging out his own moment of power because it might be the last time he performed a duty of this kind.

The documents Venning drew from the envelope crackled ominously and Oliver could fairly feel his mother's agitation. Calm down, old lady, he urged her silently, meeting her distracted gaze with a cool look. It was just as well the others were watching the solicitor, he thought drily, or they might have wondered why Stella was looking so apprehensive.

Venning cleared his throat, quickly scanning the several pages he held in his hand. Then, sonorously, and with all ceremony, he began, '''I, Griffith Henry Williams, being of sound mind—'''

'Must we drag this out?' Stella's nerve snapped at the indication that the solicitor intended to read every word of the will. Then, as if realising how unfeeling she must have sounded, she forced a strained smile. 'I'm sorry. I'm afraid I'm not as strong as I thought I was.'

Venning sniffed and looked round at the rest of them. 'Of course, of course,' he said, though whether that was an answer to her question or a confirmation of her frailty Oliver couldn't be sure. 'If no one else has any objections,' the old man added, 'I see no reason why we shouldn't—what is it they say nowadays?—cut to the chase?' He looked at Oliver. 'Perhaps your mother would like a little brandy.' He shuffled the papers between his gnarled hands. 'None of us minds waiting, I'm sure.'

'I think we'd all prefer it if you got on with it, Mr Venning.' It was Laura who spoke, and for once Stella gave her a grateful glance.

'Yes, please,' she said. 'I'll be all right.' She cast a bitter look towards Oliver. 'I don't usually drink this early in the day.'

'No, but these are exceptional circumstances,' persisted the solicitor, and Oliver found himself expelling an impatient breath.

'Please,' he said, controlling his tone with an effort, 'won't you continue, Marcus? It may be that we'll all need a drink when you're finished.'

'What?' Venning thought for a moment he was serious, and, indeed, Oliver rather thought that he was. But then the old man seemed to sense the irony behind his statement, and, clearing his throat again, he began to speak.

There were one or two small bequests, small sums of money bestowed on colleagues and acquaintances, like the landlord of the pub in the village and the doctor, who'd also been a friend. Oliver wondered if Griff had suspected that his health might be a problem. There was a comfortable legacy for his sister-in-law, too, and Aunt Nell relaxed after her name had been read.

'And now we come to the bulk of the estate.' declared Venning solemnly. 'Naturally, you are all anxious to hear how Mr Williams divided his property, and I don't intend to keep you in suspense any longer than I must. Or course, I must impress upon you that this will is legal and binding and Mr Williams thought long and hard before coming to his decision.'

'Oh, do get on with it.'

Aunt Nell was evidently getting irritated now, and Oliver

realised that the old lady still had a stake in the proceedings. If, as she evidently suspected, Stella had inherited Penmadoc, her own position in the house was hardly secure.

'Very well.' If Venning was offended by her impatience, he hid it well and, clearing his throat for the third time, he began again. '"To my wife, Stella,"' he said, glancing across the desk at her, '"I leave one half share in my house and all my personal possessions, save those articles of jewellery that were given to me by my first wife, Maggie, and which I would like my daughter, Laura, to have as a memento of the love her mother and I shared. I further bestow sufficient funds to enable my wife to continue to live at Penmadoc, if she so wishes, on the understanding that my sister-in-law, Eleanor Tenby, shall always have a home there as well. Should my wife, Stella, choose to marry again, or live elsewhere, the house will revert wholly to my daughter, Laura, as it will, in any event, at my wife's death."'

There was an audible gasp after he'd finished reading this clause of the will, though who had uttered it Oliver wasn't sure. His mother, he suspected, though it would be dangerous for her to show any surprise that this wasn't the same will she had seen. It might even have been Laura. She was certainly paler now than she'd been when she'd entered the library. Like his mother, she must have expected she knew what was in the will.

'Um...shall I go on?'

The solicitor hesitated. Oliver guessed he'd been expecting some kind of outburst from his mother, but Stella seemed too shocked to say a word. It was lucky her reaction could be attributed just as easily to the fact that she hadn't inherited *all* of Penmadoc, he reflected. But what the hell was *he* going to do now?

Realising that Venning was waiting, Oliver gave him a terse look. 'Of course,' he said, his lips tightening in sudden frustration, and the solicitor turned once again to the will.

'"To my daughter, Laura,"' he said, smiling encouragingly at her, ''I bequeath the aforementioned jewellery, as well as all my books and pictures and one half share in the home we shared for many years. Perhaps this shared responsibility will create an understanding between my wife and my daughter that was never evident in my lifetime, and I appoint my stepson, Oliver Kemp, as executor to this effect.'''

CHAPTER TEN

DESPITE Aunt Nell's pleas to the contrary, Laura left Penmadoc that afternoon. She knew there would be things to do, papers to sign, arrangements to be made, but she couldn't bear to stay in the house any longer. She needed time—and space—to come to terms with what had happened, and so long as Oliver was in the same building she knew she'd never have any peace.

Goodness knew, she hadn't had any peace since he'd kissed her. That was why she'd left the house that morning, in the hope of finding some sanctuary in the church which she'd attended as a child. But the church was full of memories, Penmadoc was full of memories, and she'd known then she had no choice but to leave.

Though not in these circumstances, she thought, after the train had deposited her at Euston station and she had hired a cab to take her to a hotel. She'd had no idea that her father might leave Penmadoc to her—or any part of it—and even the knowledge that it was Stella's home for as long as she wanted or needed it, couldn't mar the pride she felt in knowing that the house was going to remain in the family.

Her family.

Aunt Nell's family too, she acknowledged gratefully. It was good to know the old lady's position was secure as well. Although Oliver had reassured her that his mother wanted to stay at Penmadoc, she had had her doubts about Stella's intentions towards her aunt.

Her own position was much more complicated. Apart from the continuing animosity that existed between her and Stella, she didn't see how she could spend any time at Penmadoc when her work was in New York. Besides which, Stella must be furious that Griff had double-crossed her. Laura had few doubts that her stepmother had expected to inherit the house in its entirety.

As for Oliver...

But she didn't want to think about Oliver now. Oliver was still at Penmadoc, consoling his mother, no doubt, reassuring her that Laura was unlikely to make things difficult for her. He knew about her work; he'd cleverly found out all about her while they were having lunch that day. He was in the perfect position to assure his mother that she had nothing to worry about.

It was early evening by the time she'd checked into the hotel and unpacked her belongings. She'd had to choose one of the larger hotels because she didn't know the names of any of the smaller ones. But the one she'd chosen was impersonal and efficient, and she told herself that that was all she needed. After all, this wasn't a social visit. Staying here would give her time to decide what she was going to do.

Room Service provided her with a light supper. She could have gone down to the restaurant, but it was less trouble to eat in her room. Afterwards, she put aside her misgivings and phoned Aunt Nell to let her know where she was, asking her not to broadcast her whereabouts unless some sort of emergency occurred.

'You really ought to have stayed here,' Aunt Nell told her reprovingly. 'This is your house, Laura. Don't let anyone tell you any different.'

'I won't,' Laura assured her, recalling the tact that Stella hadn't said a word to anyone after the solicitor had finished reading the will. Which she might have thought was unusual, she reflected, if she hadn't been so stunned herself.

'Well, you see they don't,' declared her aunt firmly. 'Who knows what that woman will try to do now? She's suffering from shock at the moment, but that won't last. And once she realises you've thwarted her plans she won't be very pleased.'

Laura sighed. 'What plans?' she asked wearily. 'Aunt Nell—'

'Her plans to sell Penmadoc, of course.' Her aunt clicked her tongue. 'Don't tell me you thought that she'd want to stay in the village after Griff had no say in the matter? For pity's sake, girl, she's been hankering after moving to Cardiff or suchlike for years.'

Laura's eyes widened. 'But I thought—'

'Yes? What did you think? That she and your father lived an idyllic life together?'

'Well—'

'Oh, Laura, didn't he tell you? I should have known he'd be too proud to admit it. He and you-know-who haven't shared a bedroom for years.'

Laura sat down abruptly on the side of the bed. She'd had no idea that there was anything wrong between her father and Stella. And yet... She remembered again how unusually cheerful he'd seemed last summer when she'd seen him in London. She'd been wondering whether he'd been hiding the fact that his heart was failing. She'd never dreamt he might have been hiding something else.

'So—what are you implying, Aunt Nell?' she returned at last, not sure where this was heading or even if she wanted to go there. She took a deep breath. 'Was there—is there someone else? Is that what you're saying?'

The old lady seemed to draw back from making such a damning accusation. 'All I'm saying is that you shouldn't take too much for granted,' she said, choosing her words with care. 'Stella will have her own agenda. You can be sure of it. Things aren't always the way they seem, you know.'

Laura stifled a groan. It was obvious her aunt wasn't prepared to make it easy for her. If she wanted to know any more, she would have to find out for herself. It crossed her mind that this might be Aunt Nell's way of getting her back to Penmadoc, but for the next few days she was determined to stay where she was.

She rang Conor's uncle—and her employer—a couple of days later. Matthew Neill was sympathetic about her situation, but it was obvious he wanted her in New York. 'The last time I looked at your desk, I couldn't see it for a mountain of paper,' he remarked drily. 'It's been over a week, Laura. When are you coming back to work?'

'Only just over a week,' Laura pointed out exactly. 'And he was my father, Matt. I need a little time to settle his affairs.'

'Yeah.' She could almost see his scowl. 'And I suppose inheriting this house rather complicates things, doesn't it? Are you planning on selling it? I can't see that it's gonna be of any use to you.'

Laura gave a rueful shake of her head. Where property was concerned, Matt's opinion was that you either lived in it or you sold. He'd handled the sale of the brownstone when she and Conor had split up, thus saving her any heartache, and found her the loft apartment in Greenwich Village which she presently enjoyed.

'It's not mine to sell,' she said now, although that was just a prevarication. Even if Stella was prepared to sell in exchange for half the profits, Laura wouldn't have wanted to get rid of the old house. 'I've told you: my father left half to my stepmother. I couldn't ask her—or my aunt—to find somewhere else to live.'

'Well, you're gonna have to make a decision,' said Matthew flatly. 'I need you here. Like I said before, the work's piling up.' He broke off for a moment. 'There's not something you're not telling me, is there, sweetie? You've not met some man from your past who wants you to stay in England?'

'No!' Laura's response was convincingly vehement, but she couldn't help the unwilling thought that his suspicions weren't that far from the truth. 'I'll be back,' she said. 'Next week at the latest. Until then, you're just going to have to manage without me.'

Nonetheless, Matthew's words had unsettled her. What with Aunt Nell's intimations on the one hand and his insinuations on the other, it was well nigh impossible for her to relax. Was she so transparent, she wondered, that Conor's uncle could actually sense what she was thinking over the wires? Or was she simply attributing him with extra perception because of her own guilt?

Whatever, when she climbed into bed that night, she was hardly surprised when her thoughts drifted back to that fatal evening. The evening when she'd taken her courage into her hands and gone to Oliver's room. Looking back on it now, she didn't know how she'd had the nerve to do it. It was ironic really because she knew she would never have had the courage to do it now.

But then, it was the events that had happened during and after that evening that had made such a difference to her life, she reflected. Without the memories of the past, she wouldn't be the woman she was today. Or feel such a lingering hatred towards Oliver, she told herself, though hatred was not what she'd felt when he'd kissed her the night of her father's funeral. She'd wanted him then; there was no point in denying it; just as much as she'd wanted him fourteen years ago...

It had been a hot day. It had been an unusually hot summer, and the farmers who ran their sheep on the hills around Penmadoc were crying out for rain. But that night, at least, there was the promise of a storm in the offing, and all evening there'd been the rumble of thunder in the distance.

It was the threat of the storm that had made Laura feel restless. Or so she'd told herself. That, and the fact that she'd spent the afternoon watching Oliver training with the school athletics team. She'd felt such pride when he'd returned to her side after every event, flopping down on the grass beside her, to the envy of many of the older girls.

But it wasn't just pride that had caused her to feel so unsettled. It was the lean strength of his long body as he'd lounged beside her that had made her aware of him in a totally physical way. The sweat beading on his forehead, running like raindrops down the smooth skin of his torso had fascinated her, and she'd wanted to press him back into the grass and taste his essence for herself.

Something of what she'd been feeling must have shown in her eyes because Oliver had noticed. 'Hey, don't look at me like that, baby,' he said, 'or you might get more than you bargained for.'

'Could I?' she responded tartly, though her cheeks burned with colour, and Oliver covered her hand where it lay on the grass and pressed his thumb into her palm.

Even that small intimacy set off a series of sensual explosions inside her. Her stomach quivered with an unfamiliar excitement, and she desperately wanted to explore further. She was trembling with the strength of her emotions, and she hoped he might teach her what it meant.

But Oliver was called back to the field at that moment and when he returned Laura had no opportunity to rekindle their earlier intimacy. A group of his fellow athletes came with him and they were keen to go down to the pub to quench their thirst with lemon chasers. Some of the older boys were already eighteen and there was a lot of horseplay about who was going to have a beer and who wasn't. At sixteen, Laura felt very much the outsider, and although she went with them it was the older girls now who held centre stage.

They all walked home together, however, but although she and Oliver covered the last few yards alone all he wanted to talk about was the fact that he hoped to continue with his athletics when he went to university. He was still high from the success he'd had in the last race he'd entered and when they arrived at Penmadoc he went at once to take a shower.

Laura hoped that her father and Stella might be going out that evening. But the prospect of the storm made everybody edgy, and after exchanging words with her husband over the fact that she'd overspent on her allowance again her stepmother announced that she intended to take a bath and didn't

want to be disturbed. Oliver disappeared up to his room as
Laura and Aunt Nell were doing the dishes, and as her father
always retired to his study when he was upset she spent the
rest of the evening on her own.

She went to bed at eleven o'clock and spent the next hour
trying to make sense of the Margaret Atwood novel that had
previously held her interest. But the words all ran together
and, after turning several pages without having the faintest
idea what she'd read, she put the book aside.

She couldn't stop thinking about Oliver. She didn't know
why exactly, but somehow that afternoon their relationship
had taken a more serious turn and she badly wanted to talk
to him about it. She wanted to know if he felt the same, if
he'd experienced any of the feelings that had troubled her
since he'd touched her, or whether she'd only imagined the
sudden intimacy between them.

She might be only sixteen, she thought, but she wasn't
naïve. She knew what went on between a man and a woman,
and she'd had first-hand knowledge of how strong that at-
traction could be. Surely her father could never have become
involved with Stella so soon after her mother's death if he
hadn't been irresistibly attracted to her. Although she still
found that hard to stomach, Laura had learned to be philo-
sophical about something she couldn't change.

Even so, she couldn't believe that the way she felt about
Oliver bore any resemblance to what went on between her
father and Stella. They were so much older, for one thing.
She wasn't even sure if they did 'it' any more.

She'd learned what 'it' was when she was about thirteen,
and since then it had become a regular topic of conversation
among her contemporaries at the comprehensive. Some of
the girls even claimed to have done 'it' themselves, but Laura
doubted that many of them had actually taken the risk. Even
in this age of sexual freedom, most girls would fight shy of
inviting an unwanted pregnancy and all that it would mean.

Nevertheless, the idea of making love with Oliver was a

captivating thought. Remembering his lean brown torso and the way his stomach muscles rippled beneath his taut skin caused a shiver to feather down her spine. He was hairy, too; not a lot, just a light sprinkling on his chest and over his arms and legs that deepened his tan. But it was the place where it arrowed down below his navel that fascinated her. She was curious to know if he had hair between his legs.

Her thoughts troubled her. She'd always felt a certain contempt towards girls who talked constantly about sex and what it meant to them. Although she'd loved Oliver for years, she'd never imagined herself falling *in love* with him. Yet there didn't seem to be any other reason for the way she was feeling. Or for the tingling awareness that was prickling her skin.

It was upsetting, but it was also exciting, and she knew she would never get to sleep if she didn't share her feelings with someone else. She'd never had a really close girlfriend, and there was no way she could discuss it with her father. As for Stella, well, she knew exactly how her stepmother would react if she confessed her feelings to her.

There was only one solution: late as it was, she would have to hope that Oliver wasn't asleep. He had a computer in his room, and she knew he sometimes played games on it for hours. So much so that his mother had threatened to deduct the cost of the electricity he was using from his allowance.

It was rather daunting to leave her bedroom. She entertained the nightmare of what she would do if someone saw her going into Oliver's room. As well as her stepmother's disapproval, she doubted it would find much sympathy with her father. As far as Griff Williams was concerned, she was still his little girl.

Despite the fact that she was wearing her dressing gown, the corridors were cold and just a little spooky. Although she used to tease Oliver that Penmadoc was haunted, she'd never really believed it herself. Until tonight. Her feet were bare and she shivered uneasily. It was so easy to imagine she wasn't alone.

It was quite a relief to reach Oliver's room. There was no sign of a light under the door, but he didn't always use the light when he was working on his computer, for obvious reasons. However, when she took her courage in both hands and opened the door, the sight that met her startled eyes caused a sudden constriction in her throat.

Oliver was there, all right, but he wasn't working on his computer. He was in bed, asleep, the sheet which was all that had covered him kicked down around his ankles. He'd once teased Laura that he wore nothing to sleep in. She'd never dreamed she'd find out that it was true.

Hardly knowing what she was doing, Laura stepped into the room, allowing the door to close behind her. Somehow her hand found the handle and prevented any sound from escaping into the corridor, and then she sank back against the panels, gazing open-mouthed at her stepbrother's reclining form.

The curtains were open, and moonlight streamed down on to his naked body. In the silvery light, his skin had an unearthly sheen, like the pelt of a selkie, that mythical creature that was said to haunt the waters around Scotland and which assumed human form to seduce a woman. And seeing him, like this, seduced Laura's sensibilities, so that instead of getting out of there as she knew she should she pushed herself away from the door and approached the bed.

She stood for several minutes, just looking down at him, and then the temptation to touch got the better of her, and, sinking down on to her knees, she stretched out her hand and ran her fingers over the smooth curve of his hip.

'What the hell—?'

Oliver came awake with a start, frightening Laura so much that for a moment she couldn't move. She froze there, her eyes wide, like a rabbit caught in the headlights of a car, and gazed at him in total panic.

'Laura!' Although Oliver must have been as startled to find her there as she was at being caught, he recovered more rapidly, dragging the sheet up around his hips with one hand as he pushed himself up with the other. 'For God's sake, what's wrong?'

Laura's mouth was dry. 'I—I—nothing's wrong,' she protested, shocked by the awareness that his arousal had manifested itself first in a different part of his body. 'I—well, I wanted to talk to you.'

Oliver blinked and glanced at the clock on his bedside table. 'At half-past twelve?' he exclaimed disbelievingly. 'For pity's sake, what was so important that it couldn't wait until morning?'

'I—nothing.' Suddenly, Laura was convinced she had made a terrible mistake. Contrary to her beliefs, Oliver hadn't been affected by what had happened that afternoon. And why should he have been, for goodness' sake? It wasn't as if he hadn't had other girlfriends, other relationships. He'd only squeezed her hand. She'd blown what had been a purely friendly gesture right out of proportion. 'It was nothing.' She scrambled to her feet. 'I'm sorry I disturbed you.'

'Laura...'

His tone was frustrated, but she had heard enough. She'd made a total fool of herself, and she'd be lucky if he didn't tell all his friends what an idiot she was. All she wanted to do was get back to her room as quickly as possible and try and forget what she'd done.

She was fumbling for the handle of the door when his hand came over her shoulder and flattened against the panels. 'Wait,' he said huskily, his breath warm against the nape of her neck. 'Tell me why you really came to my room. I want to know.'

Laura took a deep breath. God, she thought unsteadily, he was right behind her. She could feel the heat of his body reaching out to her, enveloping her, wrapping her in the same intimacy she had felt that afternoon.

'You don't want to know,' she said in a muffled voice, but of course he did. He wouldn't have left his bed and come after her if he hadn't wanted to know exactly why she'd felt compelled to do something so out of character, so dangerous. And suddenly she knew she was in danger. But not from him; from herself.

'Tell me,' he said, his lips brushing her ear, and her stomach turned over at the unexpected tingle that caused. 'Come on, baby.' His hand left the door to curl across her throat and grip her shoulder. It took a very little pressure to bring her back against his chest. 'Talk to me.'

Laura's heart was pounding. Being close to him like this was more thrilling than she could ever have imagined, and the awareness that only the man's tee shirt she used to sleep in and her thin dressing gown were all that was between them caused a fluttering sensation in the pit of her stomach.

'Laura...' His voice had thickened, and his free hand came around her waist. Whether by accident or design—she was too bemused to decide which—his fingers slid beneath the opening of her robe, gripping her hip and pulling her even closer. 'Dammit, Laura, talk to me. Tell me you didn't come here because of what I said this afternoon. I was a fool. I shouldn't have—teased you like that. It wasn't fair.'

Laura swallowed the lump that rose in her throat at his words. Her excitement dissolved into quivering humiliation, but when she would have dragged herself away from him he muttered an oath and held on to her.

'Don't,' he groaned, his hand sliding possessively across her abdomen, and as he held her there against him she felt the unmistakable hardening of his sex against her bottom.

Then, when she was half afraid her shaking legs were going to give out on her, he turned her round and brought her fully against him. Laura's eyes were wide with wonder when she looked up into his face, and as if some lingering twinge of conscience still troubled him Oliver lifted one hand to cup her cheek. 'You know this is crazy, don't you?' he said unsteadily, and she realised that what he'd said before hadn't been the truth. He hadn't been teasing her that afternoon. He'd been as aroused by what had happened as she had and he'd only said what he had to try and influence a situation that was rapidly moving out of control. He uttered a harsh sound. 'Tell me to stop.'

'Why should I?' she asked, her hands sliding up his chest to grip the dark hair that tangled at his nape. The power she sensed she had over him was tantalising. 'That's not what you really want to hear.'

'You don't know what I really want,' he replied thickly, his fingers tightening on her chin, causing her mouth to open and emit laboured panting breaths.

'Don't I?' Somehow, she pulled her face free of his hand. 'I'm not a child, Oliver.'

'I wonder.' He gritted his teeth, but his hand moved almost compulsively to the back of her neck, tilting her face up to his. 'I wonder,' he muttered again, and this time he couldn't stop himself. With the tumult of his emotions darkening his eyes, he bent his head and covered her mouth with his.

Laura's knees buckled and she clutched his shoulders to prevent herself from slipping to the floor. There was such a wealth of emotion in his kiss and although she was by no means experienced when it came to making out with boys she instantly recognised the difference between Oliver's love-making and the amateurish fumblings she'd known before. For one thing, Oliver knew exactly what he was doing and, for another, for the first time in her life she wasn't repulsed by it.

'God, Laura,' he said hoarsely, when he released her mouth to seek the sweetly scented skin of her shoulder. His fingers peeled back the layers of cloth to expose her creamy flesh, brushing aside the tendrils of red-gold hair that had escaped from the braid she'd worn to sleep in and kneading her quivering skin. 'I want you. You know that. But not like this. It isn't right.'

Laura's confidence wavered for only a moment. 'It is for me,' she told him fiercely, winding her arms around his neck and lifting one leg to caress his calf with her heel. She'd seen that done in a play she'd watched on television and she was amazed to find it stimulated her just as much as it apparently stimulated him. 'I want you. How can that be wrong?'

'God knows,' he groaned, his hands sliding down her back to cup her bottom and lift her against him. 'Perhaps it isn't,' he added, as if trying to convince himself, and then, because she wrapped her legs around him, he gave up the unequal struggle and carried her to the bed.

For a moment after he'd pushed off her dressing gown and peeled her tee shirt over her head, Laura knew a moment's panic. His sheets were cool at her back and they caused a brief spasm of sanity to chill her blood. But it didn't last long. When Oliver knelt beside her and bent to take one erect nipple into his mouth, she thought she was in heaven. She was half afraid she would die from the pleasure his darting tongue evoked.

Time was suspended as he ran his hands over her body. She had always thought she was too tall and too lean, but evidently he didn't agree with her. There was genuine satisfaction in the eyes that met and mated with hers, and she found herself moving instinctively with him, arching her body and spreading her legs in a way that at any other time would have mortified her soul.

But there was no shame with Oliver, no inhibitions when he straddled her and invited her to touch him. His shaft was hot and hard and incredibly smooth, like steel beneath soft velvet. But, in spite of his eagerness to share his excitement with her, when her slim fingers closed around him, he moaned aloud.

'I can't—I can't wait,' he said in a strangled voice, and with a groan of anguish he came into her, slowly at first and then with an unrestrained eagerness he couldn't deny. Her muscles froze at first and then expanded to accommodate him. She felt as if it was never going to end, and she stifled a cry.

She'd been prepared for it to hurt, but what she'd not been prepared for was that after that initial agony she would begin to enjoy it. The girls at school, who had been so keen to share their experiences with her, had evidently never had a lover like Oliver. His skill and consideration soon had her moving with him. Moving willingly, instinctively, reaching for the seemingly unattainable release of the emotions he was building inside her. His lean body quickened, stroking in and out of hers with an ease and slickness that had her clinging to him helplessly. Her nails dug into his shoulders, and she wrapped her legs around him, little breathless cries issuing from her throat.

And then what had seemed to be impossible happened. Almost simultaneously, he came into her with such force that she thought she might not be able to take him after all. But she could; she did; his groan of satisfaction proved it, mingling with the cry she uttered as a devastating wave of pleasure spread throughout her body.

She wanted to weep. What had happened had been so— so beautiful, and Oliver's still shuddering body lying on top of hers gave her a feeling of real contentment. She was a woman now; in every way. She loved Oliver, and he loved her. Nothing anyone said or did could change their feelings for one another.

She'd been so wrong. Laura acknowledged that now with a shiver of distaste. What had happened afterwards had been so awful, so ugly. She couldn't even think of it without feeling a surge of nausea in her throat.

Predictably, it was Stella who had ruined everything for them. No, not for *them*, she amended bitterly. For her. The way Oliver had behaved after that night had seemed to confirm everything his mother had claimed. But when her stepmother had burst into the room and found them Laura had been too bemused to think coherently, blinking into the harsh electric light like a mole that had just been dug out of its hole.

And that was how she felt: shocked and ashamed that Stella should have been the one to find them. Her contorted face had destroyed the sweet intimacy she and Oliver had shared, and how she'd kept from screaming her outrage Laura never knew.

Of course, Stella had had some justification for her anger. This was her home and they had abused the trust she'd put in them. Laura acknowledged that, acknowledged that her stepmother must hate the fact that it was she who had been responsible for Oliver abusing that trust. But what she couldn't forgive was the fact that Oliver had conspired with his mother to keep what had happened between themselves.

The threatening storm had apparently kept Stella awake, too. The heat and humidity had made her restless, and she'd been on her way downstairs to get herself a drink when she'd heard Laura's faint cries.

At the time, Laura remembered, she'd been only too glad that it hadn't been her father who'd found them. As she scrambled out of Oliver's bed, dragging the folds of her dressing gown over her nakedness, behaving like the frightened mouse she must have appeared, Stella had had an easy target. It wasn't until later that she'd discovered that her stepmother's reasons for not betraying her to her father had had less to do with saving her from certain punishment than with stopping her son from making what she'd seen as the biggest mistake of his life.

God knew what she'd said to Oliver after Laura had left the room. Laura had thought she was making things easier by getting out of there. It was only afterwards that she'd realised that by giving in to Stella's demands then she had created a precedent that had never been reversed.

It had been comparatively easy for her stepmother to see that Laura had no further opportunity to be alone with Oliver before he left for Europe. As Laura hadn't even known he was thinking of going, she'd been prepared to wait and bide her time, sure that sooner or later Oliver himself would arrange for them to be together.

But it hadn't happened. She'd awakened one morning to be told that Oliver had left for Dover the night before. There'd been no farewell, not even a message to say how sorry he was that things had turned out as they had, and because her father had known nothing about what had happened there'd been no way she could share her feelings with him.

Laura turned and punched her pillow now, wishing it was Oliver's head. How could she have allowed him to kiss her just a few days ago? she wondered painfully. How could she have let him get close enough to her to even think that she'd welcome his treacherous caress? He hadn't changed. He was just as two-faced now as he'd been then, only now it was some other girl who was being deceived.

Poor fool!

Laura sniffed and settled down again, but her mind wouldn't let her rest. Not yet. Oliver's leaving for Europe hadn't been the end of the story, as she knew only too well. A few weeks later, when her period was late, she had had another reason to regret her recklessness.

For over a month, she'd been in a state of panic, not knowing what to do, where to turn. The idea of confiding her secret to a stranger didn't bear thinking about, and Dr Evans was a friend of her father's. How could she tell him?

And then it was all over. One day, as she was cleaning out her room, trying to imagine what she'd do if her father disowned her, she'd felt a cramping pain in her stomach. It had been worse than any of the monthly cramps she'd had before, and she'd barely made it to the bathroom before she'd felt a gushing wetness between her legs.

The ugliest part of it all was that Stella had found out about that, too. Her stepmother had come looking for her and found Laura trying to erase any trace of what had happened from the bathroom floor. She'd been so pitiful, Laura remembered bitterly. She'd actually been crying over losing the baby, when what she should have been doing was jumping for joy.

But at least Stella's finding out had enabled her to handle the situation without involving Dr Evans. Her stepmother, now she came to think of it, had been amazingly knowledgeable about the miscarriage, reassuring her she had nothing to worry about, helping her to cope with her loss. In fact, Laura belatedly wondered whether Stella herself hadn't lost a baby. It did seem unusual, that having had Oliver when she was just a teenager, she should have gone—what? Thirty years?—without getting pregnant again.

But Laura didn't want to think of the connotations of that suspicion. And at the time she'd been so eager to put it all behind her, she hadn't looked beyond her own mistake. Even Stella's warning that if she told anyone else about it she would tell her father had seemed justifiable recompense for her stepmother's silence. She hadn't thought that her father might have blamed someone else.

Of course, in the weeks that followed, she'd realised why Stella had been so helpful, why she'd been so willing to hush it up. She hadn't wanted her precious son to hear about it. As always, she'd been protecting Oliver, making sure he didn't get bogged down in unwanted guilt.

Unfortunately, it had always been there between her and her stepmother, and she supposed it always would. That was why their relationship had never changed. She knew her father had hoped that as she grew older they'd have more in common. But Laura had never been able to put the past behind her and Stella had never let her forget.

That was why she'd refused to come back to Penmadoc after her university days were over, why she'd jumped at the chance to marry Conor Neill, even though she'd known that she didn't love him as she should. She'd wanted to get away, as far away as possible, and with the width of the Atlantic between her and Oliver she had hoped to find a better life.

And she had, she assured herself fiercely. All right, her marriage hadn't worked out, but that had been as much Conor's fault as hers. They'd wanted different things from the relationship, and she'd been unable to give him the understanding he deserved.

All the same, seeing Oliver again had been a daunting experience. She had thought she would be able to handle it better than she had. She hated the thought that he might think he'd got to her—even if he had...

CHAPTER ELEVEN

'ARE you all right, Mr Oliver?'

Thomas Grayson paused in the action of removing Oliver's plate, looking down at the half-eaten pasta with some concern. Since his employer had returned from Wales two days ago, he'd barely touched his food and the old man was getting worried abut him.

'Yeah, I'm fine.' Oliver lay back in his chair and looked up at Thomas with resigned complacence. 'I guess I'm still adjusting to the change of circumstances. I'm not used to sitting around all day, doing nothing. Going down into that ravine was pretty exhausting, I can tell you. Nothing like working in a comfortable studio, with every technological advantage at your fingertips.'

Thomas settled the plates on his arm and then pulled a wry face. 'It's been almost three weeks since you got back from Malaysia, Mr Oliver. You can't still be suffering from jet lag. I don't buy that.'

'Buy?' Oliver arched his dark brows humorously. 'Since when have you been using language like that?'

'Don't try to dodge the issue, Mr Oliver.' Thomas pressed his thin lips together. 'There is something wrong, isn't there?' He took a breath. 'Should I know about it?'

'If you mean, am I suffering from some fatal disease that I'm not telling you about, then forget it. I'm as fit as a flea, as far as I know.'

'Then why—'

'I'm not hungry, right?' Oliver was getting impatient now. 'I—had a burger at lunchtime. End of story.'

'That was at least six hours ago—'

'Thomas, enough. I know you mean well, but I do know when I'm hungry and when I'm not. And right now I'm not.'

'Very well.'

Barely concealing his disapproval, Thomas left the room and, stifling an oath, Oliver got to his feet and followed him. Entering his study, he went straight to the wet bar and poured himself a generous measure of Scotch, not feeling any release of tension until the single malt had invaded his bloodstream. Then, as its heat eased the grinding stiffness in his bones, he breathed a weary sigh.

But, dammit, it was a bad job if he was admitting that he needed alcohol just to function normally. What the hell was the matter with him? Thomas was right. He was different. But how different he had yet to find out.

Thomas appeared in the doorway as he was finishing the Scotch. 'Will you be wanting pudding, Mr Oliver?' he asked stiffly, his tone still showing his disapproval, and Oliver set down his empty glass and shook his head.

'Not right now,' he said, injecting a note of apology into his voice. 'I—I think I'll go out. I promised Guy McKenna I'd show him the rough proofs as soon as they were available. And a lot of them are done.'

But that was another source of frustration to him. Although he'd been back from Wales for over two days, he'd done very little work. Most of the film he'd shot in the Kasong Gorge hadn't even been processed, and if he did intend to see Guy McKenna it would be to apologise for the delay.

Of course, he knew McKenna would understand. It wasn't every day that there was a death in the family. And if his restlessness owed less to the actual bereavement and more to the knowledge of the will his mother had taken from Griff's safe, McKenna wasn't to know about it.

But he had yet to decide what he was going to do about it. He didn't even know if the will was legal, though it had been signed and witnessed by two people who, even though their names were unfamiliar to him, were obviously people Griff had trusted.

His mother had demanded he destroy it. And it would be a simple matter to do so. No one appeared to know about the second will; certainly not Laura, who had left Penmadoc the same afternoon the will was read without even saying goodbye. She clearly didn't want to live at Penmadoc, not immediately, at least, and it would come to her automatically if his mother married again.

Or died, he added, with rather less indifference. The idea of Stella shuffling off this mortal coil was not quite so easy to face. She was his mother, dammit. Whatever she'd done, whatever secrets she'd kept from him, she had been Griff's wife. Didn't he owe it to her to let her live in the home they'd shared for the past twenty years?

But for some reason Griff had changed his will, and Oliver could only wonder at the feelings that had caused such a change of heart. What had Stella done? What lie had Griff caught her out in? What betrayal had been so bad that the old man had decided she didn't deserve to stay at Penmadoc?

In the days following Laura's departure, he'd found no answers. His mother had said and done nothing to arouse his suspicions, and Aunt Nell had been as predictably reticent about her feelings as she was about Laura's whereabouts. If she knew where her niece was, she wasn't saying, and Oliver had wondered if the kindest thing of all wouldn't be to leave the situation as it was. Goodness knew, he didn't want to be the one to drive his mother out of Penmadoc. But he also knew he'd be betraying everything he'd ever believed in if he allowed her to have her way, and until the situation was resolved he supposed he'd go on having sleepless nights.

That was why he'd brought the will back to London with him, along with the key to the safe. Although his mother had assured him that she wouldn't attempt to tamper with her husband's papers again, Oliver was of the opinion that it was wise not to put temptation in her way.

Which was much the same thing as not trusting her, he acknowledged drily, thinking of the will locked securely in the drawer of his desk. But one way or another it was down to him, and until he'd had a chance to tell Laura he was making no promises he couldn't keep.

'If you say so, Mr Oliver.'

Thomas's disapproving response brought him to an abrupt awareness of where he was. Clearly, the man was not in the mood to be placated by a few words and Oliver wondered when he'd started down this track. When Griff died, he reminded himself grimly, refusing to admit that meeting Laura again had done more to upset the comfortable little niche he'd made for himself than anyone—or anything—else.

However, before either of them could say anything more, the phone rang. Thomas arched a brow, a silent enquiry as to whether he should answer it, but on the off chance that it could be important Oliver crossed to the desk and picked up the receiver himself. He needed the diversion, he thought. There wasn't a cat in hell's chance that it might be Laura.

'Oliver!' Natalie's voice sounded shrill and unfamiliar. 'Oliver, it's me! Guess where I am?' Then, without waiting for an answer, she pressed on. 'I'm here, at Heathrow. The shoot's been cut short because two of the girls were taken ill so I'm back earlier than I expected. Isn't that great? Have you missed me?'

'I— Sure.' Oliver raised his eyes to Thomas's and gave an imperceptible shrug of his shoulders. 'That's—wonderful, Natalie.' He struggled to inject a more positive note into his voice, which was difficult when he'd barely thought of his girlfriend for the past three weeks. 'You—just caught me, actually. I was on my way out when you rang.'

'Out?' Natalie sounded less than cordial now. 'I tell you I've just flown more than four thousand miles to be with you and all you can say is that you're on your way out. Come on, Oliver. You can't be serious.'

'I'm afraid I am.' Oliver stifled a sigh, reflecting with some irony that he was in danger of alienating all the people he cared about in his life. He'd already had a blazing row with his mother when she'd discovered he'd taken the safe key with him. Did he really need any more aggravation? He strove for an upbeat response. 'It's good to hear your voice again, Nat. Did you have a good trip?'

'Do you care?' Natalie didn't attempt to hide her irritation. 'I was going to suggest you might like to come out to the airport to pick me up, but I suppose you're too busy. I'll have you know we left the island at dawn just so we could connect with this morning's Concorde from New York. I'm cold and I'm tired. I just want to go home and have a shower. I had thought I might have it with you.'

Oliver groaned. 'Look, Nat—'

'Don't try to humour me, Oliver. Not when you can't even put off whatever it is you were going to do to see the woman you're supposed to love. Do you realise it's been almost a month since we were together?'

Well, near enough, thought Oliver, knowing better than to show surprise. 'Yeah, I know, but—'

'But you're not going to change your mind, are you? I sometimes wonder if you care about me at all.'

Oliver had been wondering that, too, and it didn't help when Thomas, who had been pottering about the room as he spoke, turned to give him an enquiring look. 'Okay,' he said heavily, grimacing at Thomas's expression, 'forget what I said, right? I'll come. Yeah, yeah, right away. Tell me where you are.'

'Another change of plan?' asked Thomas primly as his employer put down the phone, and Oliver blew out a weary breath.

'You might say that.'

'Would you like some coffee before you leave?'

'No.' Oliver scowled. 'I'll get something at the airport.'

'The airport?' Thomas pretended not to understand.

'Yeah, the airport,' agreed Oliver, refusing to be provoked. 'Natalie's back. I'm going to pick her up.'

It was after midnight by the time Oliver left Natalie's apartment. The formalities at the airport had taken longer than he'd expected and then Oliver had had to pay a fine to rescue his Mercedes from the compound where it had been sequestered for being parked illegally. He knew he hadn't been in the best of moods as he'd driven back to town and his irritation had only been aggravated when they'd arrived at Natalie's apartment and she couldn't find her key. She'd eventually found it at the bottom of the vanity case she'd carried on to the plane, but not before Oliver had searched the car from end to end because Natalie had been convinced it had been in her handbag when she left the airport.

His refusal to accept her invitation to come in had provoked another argument but by then Oliver had been too tired to humour her. He'd promised to ring the next morning instead, climbing back into the Mercedes with a definite—and disturbing—feeling of relief.

There was a message on the pad beside the phone when he got home. Half expecting it to be from Natalie, checking that he'd gone straight home, he gave it only a cursory glance. If Thomas answered the phone while he was out, he usually left a handwritten message for his employer to read and Oliver assumed it wasn't important.

But, as he was turning away, Eleanor Tenby's name jumped out at him. Thomas always printed names in block letters, and curiosity as to why Laura's aunt might be ringing him had him reaching for the pad.

Thomas's message was short and to the point. There'd apparently been a break-in at Penmadoc that evening while Miss Tenby and his mother had both been out. As she'd been sure Laura would be upset at the news, she wanted him to get in touch with her and tell her what had happened.

The address of Laura's hotel followed and Oliver thought how ironic it was that suddenly he was permitted information that up to now had been denied him. He ought to ring her back and tell the old woman to find someone else to be her messenger boy, he thought grimly, but then the wider connotations of what had happened occurred to him and he wished Thomas had thought to ask what, if anything, had been stolen. He refused to acknowledge the treacherous suspicion that Stella might be involved.

He frowned, tearing the note off the pad and screwing it up before dropping it into the waste basket. If only he hadn't had to go out this evening, he might have been able to do something about it tonight. He wondered what time the old lady had rung. He might at least have been able to get in touch with Laura and find out what—if anything—she intended to do now.

He glanced at his watch. Whatever he was going to do would have to wait until morning. If he got to her hotel early enough, he should be able to catch her before she went out— if she was going out, that was. He had no idea how she was filling her time or indeed why she'd felt the need to leave Penmadoc as she had. He didn't flatter himself it was because of anything he'd done, although his own guilt wouldn't go away. She probably had friends in London, he assured himself firmly. Her publisher had an office here. She was probably catching up with her colleagues.

But what colleagues? he brooded, as he climbed the stairs to his second-floor suite. Male or female? And what the hell did it matter to him anyway?

Despite the assurances he'd made to himself that Laura was unlikely to leave her hotel before nine o'clock, Oliver was up and dressed by seven o'clock the next day. Surprising Thomas browsing through the morning newspapers as he sipped his first cup of tea of the day, Oliver took the opportunity to question him about the call he'd taken the night before.

'What time did she ring?' he asked, refusing the man's offer to make him coffee and pouring himself a cup of tea instead. 'Did she say if the intruder had been caught? What was taken? Your note didn't give any details.'

'Miss Tenby didn't give any details,' replied Thomas, folding the newspaper and putting it aside. 'I don't think she wanted to talk to me. All she said was that there'd been a break-in and would I ask you to deliver the news to Mrs Neill. I suppose she thought you could always ring her back if you wanted to. But my impression was that she wanted to keep the call as brief as possible.'

Oliver wondered why. Did his mother know she'd called? And, if not, why not? Why hadn't his mother rung him herself? The temptation to call Stella and ask her what was going on was appealing, but he squashed it. He preferred to see his mother's face when he was talking to her, and if that was a shameful admission—on his part—then so be it.

But that didn't stop him from ringing Laura's aunt, and, going on the supposition that his mother was unlikely to be up so early, he made the call while Thomas made him some toast.

To his relief, Aunt Nell answered the phone herself and she didn't seem surprised to learn that it was him. 'What's all this about a break-in?' he asked, deciding that she would prefer him to get straight to the point. 'What happened?'

'Have you seen Laura?' countered the old lady, not answering him, and Oliver breathed an exasperated sigh.

'Not yet,' he said flatly. 'I was hoping you might be able to give me a few more details. What was stolen?'

Aunt Nell hesitated. 'I'd rather not discuss that over the phone,' she said, after a few minutes. Then, because she seemed to realise that something more was expected of her, she added, 'I'm not sure what was taken. We—we're still checking.'

Oliver suppressed his impatience. 'But it was a robbery?' he persisted, and he heard her give a little tut of offended dignity.

'I'd rather talk to Laura, if you don't mind,' she said, and

Oliver knew a moment's impulse to ask why the devil she hadn't phoned her, then. But he supposed he could understand the old lady's reticence to discuss anything with him. Whatever had happened, it was Laura who was really involved.

'Will you be going down to Wales again?' Thomas asked, as his employer spread butter and marmalade on a slice of toast and attempted to shovel it into his mouth. 'I assume you will be going to see Mrs Neill after breakfast.'

'Right now,' said Oliver, around a mouthful of the delicious concoction. He grimaced. 'Sorry.' He swallowed the dregs of his tea. 'That was great.'

'Don't you want any more?' Thomas was dismayed.

'I'll get something later,' Oliver promised. 'Oh, and if Miss Harlowe calls—'

'I'll tell her you've had a family emergency,' said Thomas drily, and Oliver gave him a grateful grin.

'I owe you one,' he said, heading down the hall. 'I'll let you know what's going on when I know myself.'

CHAPTER TWELVE

A UNIFORMED commissionaire eyed Oliver's arrival at the West End hotel with doubtful eyes. But he was evidently used to seeing all-night partygoers arriving back at breakfast time and Oliver, in his black turtleneck sweater, black jeans and black leather jerkin, looked the part. Particularly as he hadn't taken the time to shave and the dark stubble of his beard gave him a disreputable elegance.

He supposed he should have phoned before turning up out of the blue. Crossing the marble reception hall, he approached the desk with some misgivings, but he hadn't wanted to give her the chance to ring Penmadoc to find out if anything was wrong and for his mother to exaggerate the situation. Stella would have few qualms about upsetting Laura, and until he'd spoken to her and gauged her reaction to the news he preferred to keep the reason for his visit to himself.

The receptionist was very accommodating. It helped that she recognised him, and his assertion that he'd just got back from abroad and was hoping to give his stepsister a surprise elicited the number of Laura's room without too much effort. Oliver took the lift to the sixth floor, aware that his heart was beating much faster than it should, and when he knocked at Laura's door he felt the unpleasant dampness of his palms.

Dammit, what was happening to him? he wondered irritably. He wasn't a schoolboy any longer and he'd never felt like this when he was going to meet Natalie. When he was going to meet any woman, for that matter, he conceded grimly. And Laura wasn't just any woman, she was his stepsister.

There was no response to his first knock and, gritting his

teeth, he knocked again. There didn't even seem to be any movement beyond the heavy panels, and he wondered if she was still asleep. She could be. Unlike him, she didn't appear to have suffered any after-effects from their encounter at Penmadoc, and he was half inclined to go away again and tell Aunt Nell that he hadn't been able to reach her.

The security peephole in the middle of the door mocked him. What if he was mistaken? What if she was standing at the other side of the door right now, watching him? He scowled. He didn't like the idea that he was providing entertainment for anyone. Least of all her.

He was getting paranoid, he thought impatiently. And, as he was weighing his options, he realised he could hear something beyond the wooden door. It was the sound of water running, and he guessed Laura was taking a shower. That was why she hadn't answered his knock. She hadn't heard him.

But, as the sound of the water was abruptly cut off, another thought occurred to him. He was probably being monitored on one of the hotel's security cameras. The rest of the corridor was deserted and there was no doubt that his presence was suspicious.

He sighed. He'd give it one last try. If she didn't open the door this time, he was going to go downstairs and find a courtesy phone. The last thing he needed was to be arrested for loitering with possible intent.

He felt self-conscious as he knocked again. Being aware of the camera made everything that much harder and he breathed a sigh of relief when he heard movement in the room beyond. There was a nerveracking moment when he thought she'd looked through the peephole and decided not to let him in, but then the lock clicked and the door opened.

She didn't immediately say anything at all. She just stood there, wrapped in one of those chunky towelling bathrobes that hotels provided for their guests, a towel attempting to hold the red-gold tangle of her wet hair in check. It wasn't succeeding. Curling strands clung damply to her flushed cheeks and were a vivid contrast to the white collar of her robe.

'Hi,' he said, when she said nothing, still aware of those security cameras. 'May I come in?'

'Why?'

Wrong answer.

Oliver heaved a sigh and glanced up and down the corridor again. 'Because our conversation is being monitored,' he said evenly. 'I've been banging on this door for the past five minutes and the management is becoming suspicious.'

'I was in the—'

'Shower. Yeah. I can see that.' He couldn't prevent his eyes from seeking their own appraisal and his lips took on a sardonic slant. 'Well? Are you going to risk being responsible for one of your closest relatives getting arrested?'

Laura's lips had tightened at the searching penetration of his gaze but she didn't contradict his interpretation of their relationship. 'I suppose you'd better come in, then,' she said, stepping aside, and Oliver moved gratefully beyond anyone's analysis but hers.

Laura waited until his shoulder had taken the weight of the door and then scooted quickly back into the bathroom. By the time Oliver had closed the outer door, the bathroom door was closed, too, and he expelled an aggravated breath. What now?

'I want to talk to you, you know,' he said, putting his face close to the panels. 'You can't stay in there for ever.'

Silence greeted this announcement, and he was just about to demand that she stop behaving like an idiot and come out of there when the door opened and Laura's face appeared.

'What do you want to talk to me about?'

'Come out and I'll tell you,' said Oliver, annoyed to find that, far from being angry with her, he was fighting a totally different kind of emotion. He walked determinedly into the room beyond the dressing area and turned to face her. 'Have you heard from your aunt?'

For once, he must have said the right thing. Wrapping the folds of the bathrobe closer about her, Laura left the comparative safety of the bathroom and came further into the bedroom. She was barefoot, he noticed, and that didn't help his rampant libido. Nor did the fact that the curtains were still drawn against the dull twilight of early morning, and the only illumination came from the lamps beside the queen-size bed.

'Why would I have heard from Aunt Nell?' she asked, obviously still wary of him, and Oliver scowled.

'Well—she rang me last night.'

'You?' Evidently, that surprised her.

'Yes, me.' Oliver endeavoured not to feel affronted by her reaction. 'There are obviously times when I have my uses.'

Laura rolled her lips inward. 'Go on.'

'Well…' There was no easy way to say it. 'Penmadoc was broken into yesterday evening.'

'No!' Laura's face paled. 'Oh, God—what was taken?'

'I've no idea,' replied Oliver. 'The old lady didn't want to discuss it with me. She just wanted me to break the news to you. I suppose she thought you'd be upset.'

But had that been her only motivation? Oliver couldn't help thinking that Laura was not some frail blossom, after all. All right, she had just lost her father, but was that a good enough reason for Aunt Nell to involve him?

Laura shook her head. 'I can't believe it,' she said. 'Why would anyone want to break into Penmadoc?'

'Why does anyone want to break in anywhere?' asked Oliver a little drily. 'People die and unwittingly draw attention to themselves. Perhaps the thief, whoever he was, wanted to see what was on offer.'

But he didn't truly believe that. With its forbidding stone walls and long narrow windows, Penmadoc didn't invite intruders. On top of that, anyone watching the house would know that there was usually someone at home, and for the robbery—if it was a robbery—to take place on the very evening that both his mother and Eleanor Tenby were out was quite a coincidence.

'And Aunt Nell didn't tell you anything more than that?'

'No.' Oliver regarded her with rueful eyes. 'So...' He drew a breath. 'What are you going to do about it?'

'Well, I suppose I'd better give her a ring.'

Oliver frowned. 'Is that wise? I wouldn't have thought you'd want to discuss anything with my mother.'

'Your mother?' Laura looked confused. 'I thought you said Aunt Nell rang you.'

'She did.' Oliver sighed. 'But if you ring the house, can you be sure Aunt Nell will answer?'

Of course she couldn't, and Laura made a *moue* with her lips. 'So what do you think I should do?' she asked, with some reluctance.

'Well, I think the old lady expects you to go down there,' Oliver declared evenly.

'Do you think so?'

Laura looked thoughtful, holding the lapels of her robe together with a nervous hand. The action forcibly reminded Oliver that she was probably naked underneath, her skin as flushed and creamy as the delicate flesh of her throat.

'I think so,' he muttered now, feigning interest in the toes of his boots. He rocked back on his heels and then forward again. 'Well—if you want a lift, let me know.'

'A lift?'

She looked doubtful and he cursed himself for getting involved again. 'Yeah,' he said flatly. 'I guess I ought to go and see how Ma's taking it.' Among other things.

'Oh, I see.' She took an involuntary backward step as if he'd actually invaded her space. 'You're going, too.' She swallowed. 'Well, I'll probably be leaving after you.'

'Will you?' Oliver allowed himself to look at her now, stoking the anger he felt at the casual way she'd dismissed his offer in an effort to stem the flare of desire her slender frame evoked. 'How do you know when I'll be leaving? Did I say?'

'No.' The colour in her cheeks deepened a little. 'But— well, I'm sure you have better things to do than wait for me.'

'What you mean is, you'd rather not come with me,' retorted Oliver tersely, not knowing why he was making such a thing of it. 'Why don't you come right out and say it? What's the matter, Laura? Are you scared of being alone with me? Are you afraid you won't be able to trust yourself?'

Laura's jaw dropped. 'In your dreams,' she muttered in a muffled voice, turning away, and although he knew he was being all kinds of a fool for prolonging this Oliver reached out and grasped her shoulder.

'I used to be,' he reminded her, swinging her round to face him, and although he felt a pang of self-reproach when she flinched he didn't let her go.

'In my nightmares, maybe,' said Laura harshly, and he gazed at her disbelievingly as his reckless action caused the towel to tumble from her hair.

The vivid tangle of red-gold curls fell about her shoulders, and his throat constricted at the sight. She looked so young, so vulnerable, so much like the girl who'd come to his bedroom all those years ago, that he felt a familiar tightening in his groin. He'd wanted her then, and he wanted her now, no matter how stupid that might be. He wanted to take her in his arms and make love to her. Not as he'd done then, but now with all the skill and experience he'd learned over years of searching for something that he was now afraid he might have had—and lost. Only he had been too young—too arrogant—to realise it.

'Laura.' He said her name hoarsely, and, as if realising the whole tenor of the conversation had changed, she moved her head slowly from side to side.

'No,' she said, and he could hear the quiver in her voice.

'Don't say anything else. I don't want to hear it. Do you hear? I don't want to hear it.'

'Why not?' It was crazy but he couldn't stop himself. Moving closer, he let his hand slide to the back of her neck, under the warm folds of her robe. Her hair clung damply to his wrist, but he scarcely noticed. He was too intent on watching her, on watching the way her eyes widened and darkened until they looked more black than grey. 'You are afraid of me.' His thumb massaged the skin below her ear. 'You have no reason to be.'

'Don't I?'

There was a curious note in her voice but he refused to acknowledge it. 'No,' he said huskily, bending to bestow a warm kiss on the curve of her jaw. 'I only want us to be—to be—'

'Friends?' she demanded breathily, and he decided he liked the heat of her breath moistening his cheek.

'Lovers, maybe?' he offered unsteadily, hardly aware of what he was saying with the knowledge of her robe brushing the sensitive swelling between his legs. God, he was hard, he realised; hard, and aching with a need he'd never experienced before. His free hand moved to loosen the cord that held her robe in place, and when the two sides parted he caught his breath at the naked beauty he'd exposed. 'Oh, baby, you're beautiful!'

Her breasts were fuller than he remembered, two rounded globes that begged for him to weigh them in his hands. Pointed nipples drew his attention to their rose-coloured areolas, the skin fine and smooth, and as soft as silk. A narrow waist, deliciously curving hips, long, long legs that were crowned with a triangle of curls as vivid as her hair. She was perfect, he thought incredulously. How could he ever have thought otherwise?

'Satisfied now?'

The words were bitter, but they were tempered by the quaver in her voice and Oliver was not deceived. Sliding his hands beneath her robe, he slipped it off her shoulders. It pooled about their feet as he drew her towards him and he felt an exultant satisfaction as her closeness went some way to easing his aching need. 'Not nearly,' he said, rubbing his hips against her, and was gratified when her mouth parted to admit his searching tongue. 'Not nearly,' he said again against her lips. 'God, Laura, we can't let this get away from us again.'

He kissed her once more, then trailed his tongue along her jawline before dipping to press hot wet kisses on the creamy slope of her breast. He licked one swollen nipple before taking it into his mouth and sucking strongly on the tip. She jerked when he bit her and he knew she was as sensitive to his touch as he was to hers.

His hands brushed the undersides of her breasts before curving over her hips to find the provocative swell of her bottom. She couldn't prevent herself from arching towards him when his thumbs skimmed the responsive cleft that marked the nub of her spine, and he heard her catch her breath when he parted her legs and found the pulsing petals between.

'You're wet,' he said, his voice thick and triumphant, and, picking her up, he carried her to the bed.

He knew a momentary uncertainty when he saw that her eyes were open and watching him with an odd expression in their depths as he attempted to kick off his boots and unbuckle his belt all at the same time. There was a disturbing lack of emotion in her gaze, but he convinced himself that he was imagining it. She was just as aroused as he was. He'd proved that for himself.

Achieving his objective, he flung himself beside her, but as he was reaching for her she spoke. 'Are we going to have sex now?' she asked in a low voice, and his breath gushed out of his lungs in a crippling rush.

'No,' he said, when he was able to speak again. 'We're going to make love.'

'Love?' Her voice broke as she echoed his reply. 'You don't know the meaning of the word.'

Oliver's arousal subsided as quickly as it had stiffened earlier. 'What the hell—?'

'Is that why you came?' she asked, propping herself up on her elbows, seemingly indifferent to the fact that she was naked as the day she was born. 'Has there really been a break-in at Penmadoc, or was that just a way of getting in here?'

Oliver swallowed, feeling sick to his stomach. She didn't even sound like the Laura he knew any more, and he stared at her as if he couldn't believe his eyes. 'Don't be so ridiculous,' he muttered, rolling away from her so she couldn't see his flaccid sex. 'Of course there's been a break-in. Would I lie to you about something like that?'

'I don't know.' She paused. 'Would you?'

'No, I wouldn't,' he snapped, getting off the bed and keeping his back to her as he hauled on his trousers. 'Don't be stupid.'

'But is it stupid?' She spoke consideringly and he hated the way she was weighing his words before she answered. 'I suppose it begs the question of what you would lie to me about, doesn't it?' She took a breath. 'Have you lied to me, Oliver? Since I got back, I mean? I'd like to know.'

'I don't want to have this conversation,' he said heavily, wondering if he had ever felt this bad before. He didn't think so. He zipped up his trousers and fastened his belt. Then, forcing himself to turn back to her, he added, 'I've given you the message. What you choose to do about it is your decision, not mine.' He picked up his jerkin off the floor where he'd dropped it, deliberately keeping his eyes away from her still too delectable body, and started towards the door. 'I'm out of here.'

'Wait!'

Her cry arrested him, and although he desperately needed to put some space between himself and the pathetic mistake he'd just made he halted. But he didn't look back; didn't do anything except wait for her to tell him what she wanted, and he heard her scramble off the bed and the frantic tussle she had to put her bathrobe back on.

'What time are you leaving?' she asked, and now he did cast a disbelieving glance over his shoulder.

'What's it to you?'

Laura shrugged, but the deepening of colour in her cheeks showed that she was no longer as immune to any emotion as she'd appeared. 'Because—because I'd like to accept your offer of a lift, if it's still available,' she said awkwardly. 'If—if you don't want to take me, I'll understand.'

Oliver's fists clenched now. 'Oh, will you?' he said, angry that she could still stir his emotions without any apparent effort on her part. But he had to get a hold of himself, he thought. He couldn't let her see how badly he'd been affected. 'Shall we say a little over an hour?' he asked, playing her at her own game. 'I'll pick you up outside the hotel at nine o'clock.'

'All right.' Laura's tongue appeared to moisten her lips and he had to drag his gaze away from its provocative assault on his senses. She paused, and then, as he completed his journey to the door, she added, 'I'm sorry if you think I've treated you badly. I—just don't like being mauled, you see.'

CHAPTER THIRTEEN

OH, GOD, why had she said that?

As she phoned Room Service for fresh orange juice and coffee, she groaned aloud at her own stupidity. Why had she attempted to make any kind of an apology to him? He certainly didn't deserve it. Aunt Nell might have asked him to tell her what had happened—she had to accept that—but she knew her aunt wouldn't expect him to turn up at her hotel at half-past seven in the morning. He'd probably anticipated that she'd still be in bed. Had he come here with the express intention of joining her?

She paced restlessly about the room. The nerve of the man! And then to aggravate the offence by pretending he wanted to 'make love' with her. Did he think she was a total fool? Well, yes, of course he must. Why else would he have suggested such a thing? He didn't care about her; he didn't even care about his girlfriend. No, the only person he cared about was himself.

So why had she taken him up on his offer of a lift? The train timetable was lying in the drawer of the bureau so she didn't even have the excuse of not knowing what time the trains to Swansea ran. She should have let him go. Proved to him, once and for all, that she didn't need anything from him. So why hadn't she?

She sighed. The truth was, she didn't know why she had asked him to take her to Penmadoc. Unless, contrary to her vain posturings, she did still care about him. It was crazy, particularly after the way he'd treated her, but no matter what she said, what she did, she had never found the happiness with any man that she'd once known with Oliver.

Not that she intended to tell him that, she thought bitterly

145

as she hurriedly doffed the bathrobe and rummaged in the drawer for her underwear. She didn't spend a lot of time on her hair. It was still damp when she twisted it into a French braid, tendrils falling in bright curls against her pale cheeks. She wore the trouser suit she'd worn to her father's funeral, a dark blue woollen velour, teamed with a cream silk shell to highlight the neckline.

She was fastening thick-soled boots when her breakfast arrived, and she drank the orange juice and two cups of coffee while she packed a few personal items into her backpack. She only intended to take sufficient clothes to last a couple of days. The time Matthew Neill had given her was running out and unless she intended to run the risk of losing her job she had to leave for New York before the end of the week. It was not a prospect she faced with any degree of enthusiasm at the moment, but she was not naïve enough to think that she really had any alternative.

She was downstairs, informing the receptionist that she was going away for a couple of days but that she was leaving most of her belongings in her room, when Oliver came through the lobby doors. He was now wearing a black parka in place of the leather jacket and she couldn't help the unwilling thought that dark colours always drew attention to the vivid green of his eyes. He still hadn't shaved, she noticed grudgingly. But then, why should he? He didn't care what she thought of him.

'Are you ready?' he asked, crossing the floor in lithe, easy strides, and against her will Laura felt her stomach tighten in unwelcome anticipation of the journey ahead of them.

'Almost,' she said, turning back to the receptionist, but now the girl was looking at Oliver with warm, approving eyes.

'Hello again,' she said. 'Did you surprise her?' Then, glancing awkwardly at Laura, she said, 'Oh, of course, you must have. That's why Mrs Neill is checking out, I suppose.'

'I'm not checking out—'

'No, well—'

'Bethany—' Oliver had scanned the name-tag pinned to the receptionist's jacket and used the girl's name with a confidence Laura could only envy. 'Bethany very kindly gave me your room number,' he said, his eyes warning Laura not to make an argument of it. 'I told her I wanted to surprise you.' His eyes darkened. 'I guess I did.'

Her lips thinned, but she didn't contradict him. There wasn't much point, and at least it explained how he'd known where to find her. She didn't remember giving Aunt Nell the number of her room and she had wondered how he'd found out. But it had been a fleeting thing, and she'd had so much else on her mind at the time that it hadn't lingered.

'Going somewhere nice?' asked Bethany conversationally, but Laura discovered there was a limit to how much she could take.

'No,' she said abruptly, and, collecting her handbag from the desk and the backpack off the floor, she turned away.

Oliver's Jeep was parked outside. She could see it through the swing glass doors, and as she walked towards them she heard him thanking the girl for her help. She ground her teeth together in frustration, but there was nothing she could do about it. However, when he came after her and attempted to take the canvas bag from her, she held on.

'I can manage,' she said coldly, and his lips twisted in weary resignation.

'Of course you can,' he said, holding the door open for her. 'You've made that perfectly clear.'

'Well, what did you expect?' she snapped, incapable of remaining silent now that they were outside. 'I suppose you'd prefer it if I was as easy to charm as—as Bethany!'

Oliver grimaced. 'Well, now you come to mention it—'

'You—beast!'

'Hey…' He opened the passenger door for her to get into the vehicle. 'Can I help it if you're jealous?'

'Jealous!' Laura's jaw dropped as he slammed the door

behind her. Then, after he'd circled the car and got in beside her, she exclaimed, 'I'm not jealous! I—I despise you.'

'Yeah, I know.' Oliver closed his own door and adjusted the rear-view mirror. 'I just wish I knew why.'

Laura turned to stare at him, but he wasn't looking at her. He was concentrating on pulling out into the stream of traffic that made Park Lane such a busy thoroughfare, and she eventually returned her attention to the tight ball she'd made of her hands in her lap.

In fact, they didn't talk again until they'd joined the M4 heading west. At this hour of the morning the roads around the capital were busy, but once they reached the motorway the pressure was eased and traffic moved quickly along the three-lane highway. A lot of the vehicles heading towards Wales and the west were of a commercial nature, and Oliver drove almost constantly in the overtaking lane.

'All right?' he said at last, when Laura was beginning to wonder if he intended to cover the whole distance without saying a word, and she pressed her lips together and shrugged.

'Why wouldn't I be?' she countered, and this time he turned to give her an impatient look.

'Why, indeed?' he agreed, turning back to the road. 'Tell me, do you get pleasure out of being unpleasant to people in general, or is it only me who brings out the worst in you?'

Laura caught her breath. 'What did you expect?' she demanded. 'You don't exactly treat me with respect.'

'No?'

'No.'

He frowned. 'So what are we talking about here? The mistake I made in thinking you wanted me to make love to you a couple of hours ago, or am I right in thinking you're still bearing a grudge because of what happened fifteen years ago?'

'Fourteen years ago,' Laura corrected him quickly, and

then wished she hadn't when his eyes darkened with sudden understanding.

'Damn, that is what this is all about!' he exclaimed incredulously. 'My God, you said you'd got over it. That you'd forgiven me. What the hell did I do to make you hate me so much?'

Laura turned her head towards the window. 'Nothing.'

'Don't give me that.' Oliver was getting angry now; she could sense it. 'Talk to me, dammit. We used to be able to tell each other anything.'

'When we were kids,' said Laura disparagingly. 'That was a long time ago, Oliver.'

'Don't I know it? Which only makes this conversation even more incredible. I've said I'm sorry, for God's sake. I am. If I'd known it was going to foul up our relationship—' He broke off, and then added flatly, 'Hell, Laura, if it hadn't been me, it would have been someone else.'

'Someone else?' She arched a haughty brow. 'Someone else, what?'

'Don't make me spell it out,' he said harshly. 'You know exactly what I mean. That summer—you were growing up, Laura. I wasn't the only guy who couldn't take his eyes off you. You were hot. A ripe, luscious peach just waiting to be picked.'

'You bastard!'

Laura's fist connected with his midriff with more force than she guessed he would have given her credit for. It knocked the wind out of him and for a few seconds the Jeep veered dangerously out of control. But somehow he managed to hang on to the wheel, and when he could get his breath he swore angrily.

'Crazy bitch,' he choked, using the car's indicators to signal that he was leaving the motorway at the next exit. Moving into the nearside lane, he swung up the ramp into a service area and, finding a parking space, he rammed on his brakes.

Laura was already feeling some remorse for attacking him

as she had, and she knew Oliver had every right to be angry when she'd recklessly endangered both their lives. But shame, and a certain stubbornness, kept her silent, and it was left to Oliver to turn in his seat and stare at her with grim, accusing eyes.

'What the hell was that for?' he demanded, rubbing his midriff with a defensive hand. 'Can't you have a conversation without resorting to violence?'

'Not with you, no.'

Oliver blew out a frustrated breath. 'Why not?'

'I don't want to talk about it.'

'Well, I do.' Oliver was not prepared to be conciliatory. 'You either tell me what this is all about now, or you can find your own way to Penmadoc.'

Laura's lips parted. 'You wouldn't!'

'Try me,' he said flatly. 'Go ahead. Push me far enough and you'll find out.'

Laura held up her head. 'You can't threaten me.'

'I'm not threatening you.' Oliver groaned. 'Well, I am, I suppose, but not in the way you mean. I want some answers, Laura, and you're going to give them to me.'

She stiffened. 'I don't know what you're talking about.'

'Yes, you do. I'm talking about you; me; *us*. I want to know what happened to turn us from—from friends into enemies.' He sighed. 'I'd hazard a guess that this has something to do with my mother. What the hell did she tell you to turn you against me? She swore you'd understood, that you were eager to put what had happened behind you, not just for your own sake but for your father's.'

Laura's lips twisted. 'How convenient for you.'

'What's that supposed to mean?' Oliver's fist clenched on the wheel. 'Wasn't it true? Are you saying you blamed me for what happened?'

Laura bent her head. 'Not exactly.' This was getting too deep and she didn't want to go on with it. At least he'd explained why he'd never attempted to get in touch with her.

Knowing Stella as she did, she was fairly sure that she'd have conveyed an entirely contrary message to her son. 'Look, let's just say your mother and I never did see—eye to eye.'

'So you did blame me?' Oliver shook his head. 'I wish you'd written and told me.'

'Told you what?'

'How you felt, of course. I may have been pretty arrogant in those days, but I would never have hurt your feelings. God, surely you know that?'

Laura's gaze flickered towards him and back again. 'And what would you have done?' She paused. 'Come home?'

'Maybe. If you'd wanted me to.'

'Oh, right.'

'It's true.' Oliver groaned. 'I guess I'd have done most anything for you at that time. That was half the trouble. I was crazy about you. You know that.'

'Do I?'

'You should.' Oliver scowled. 'But, dammit, Laura, I knew you were too young. When Ma suggested the kindest thing might be to give you some space to grow up a little, I—well, I believed her.'

Laura took a trembling breath. 'Am I supposed to believe this?'

Oliver balled his fist and hit the wheel impatiently. 'Okay,' he said. 'I guess I wanted to believe her. That's true, too. I knew we couldn't go on seeing one another without—well, being together, and we both know where that might have led.'

'Do we?'

'Stop pretending you don't know what I'm talking about.' He sighed. 'If you'd got pregnant and had to give up school— What? What?' He saw the disbelief in her eyes. 'It could have happened. Don't look at me like that, Laura. We were lucky we got away with it as we did. Just imagine how your father would have felt if he'd found out about us that way.'

Laura expelled an unsteady breath. 'Just imagine,' she said bitterly. 'We were lucky, weren't we?'

'That's what I'm saying,' went on Oliver eagerly. But although she said nothing to contradict him, he seemed to sense her withdrawal. 'Hey,' he protested. 'Hey, are you listening to me, Laura?'

'Of course.'

But Laura wouldn't look at him now and he was forced to go on. 'I guess this means you weren't as happy about me leaving as Ma said,' he muttered, revising his opinion. 'I suppose I knew that.'

'Did you? You hid it well.'

'Yeah, well—' He raked back his hair with an impatient hand. 'I guess I was hoping I was wrong.' He shook his head. 'But of course I wasn't. I mean, you practically ignored me when I came home, and then you went off to college and married that—jerk, Neill.' His jaw compressed. 'God, you have no idea how much I hated that supercilious bastard!'

Laura sniffed. 'Conor wasn't a supercilious bastard.'

'Wasn't he?' Oliver rubbed his chin against his fist. 'He seemed that way to me. But then, I was pretty peeved with you, too. You wouldn't even talk to me. I knew you were making a mistake marrying that—marrying him,' he amended harshly. 'I wanted to tell you, I wanted a chance to make amends for what I'd done, I guess. But you just cut me dead. I wasn't proud of myself, Laura. I'd have told you that, if you'd let me. When I lost you, I lost the most precious thing in my life.'

Laura turned burning eyes in his direction. 'Oh, please—'

'I mean it.' His mouth tightened. 'You know, sometimes I've wished that you had got pregnant, after all. Yeah—' this as she gave him an incredulous look '—crazy, eh? Selfish, too. But we'd have still been together. And I missed you so much.'

'Don't say that.' Her voice broke on the words, and, realising she couldn't take much more of this without breaking down completely, she turned her head away. 'I think we'd better go.'

'Not yet.' Oliver's knuckles brushed her cheek and she realised when he sucked in his breath that he had discovered the dampness she hadn't had time to scrub away. 'You're crying,' he said, his tone deepening with concern. 'Don't cry, sweetheart. That was then. This is now. Whatever happened in the past, we can start again.'

'Can we?' She sniffed again and pushed his hand away. 'I'm afraid I don't want to.'

'I don't think you believe that any more than I do,' Oliver told her huskily. 'If we were indifferent to one another, we wouldn't be having this conversation.' He caught her chin in his hand and turned her face to his. 'Tell me I'm wrong.'

'You're wrong,' she answered fiercely, twisting away from him. 'Aunt Nell told me your girlfriend is away on some kind of photographic shoot at the moment, so I suppose you're feeling horny. Well, tough. I won't let you use me as a substitute for her.'

Oliver stared at her. 'Is that what you think I'm doing? Do you honestly believe that this whole thing is just the ravings of a sick libido?' His lips twisted. 'God, you don't pull your punches, do you?'

Laura quivered. 'Do you deny it?'

'Yes, I deny it,' he snarled. 'Natalie's back, if you must know. I picked her up from the airport last night. And if I'd been as desperate as you say I've had—what?—more than twelve hours to get it on.'

Laura moistened her lips. 'If you say so.'

'I do say so,' he grated, turning back to the wheel. 'I don't know why I'm bothering to try and justify myself to you. You're never going to believe me. You never did.'

'That's not true.'

The words were torn from her, and his fingers stilled on the ignition key. 'Yeah, right.'

'I mean it.' Now she was aware of a reluctant need to justify herself. 'For—for years I believed everything you said.'

Oliver turned his head to look at her. 'So why don't you believe me now?'

Laura let out a breath. 'Because...'

'Because what? Because fourteen years ago I did something any normal red-blooded male would have done? I'm not a saint, Laura. I have all the usual flaws and deficiencies. And when something you want is—offered to you—you don't stop to think of the consequences.'

'I know that.'

'So?'

Laura bent her head. 'You don't understand.'

'No, I bloody don't,' he said savagely. 'So why don't you enlighten me?'

'I can't.'

'Why not?'

'I just can't, that's why.' She licked her lips. 'I'm sorry.'

'You're sorry?' His eyes were tormented, and before she could anticipate what he was going to do he turned and looped a hand behind her neck, bringing her towards him. 'I'd like to make you sorry,' he muttered, and then his mouth was on hers, and there was no time to govern her response.

She melted against him, her limbs softening into helpless pliancy as his tongue plundered her mouth. Fire, hot and purifying, spread from his lips to hers, and when his hand slipped beneath her jacket she couldn't prevent the instinctive need to arch her body against his. Her silk shell was easily freed from her waistband and when his thumb brushed the swollen tip of her nipple she felt a groan of pleasure rising in her throat.

Wherever he touched, her skin came alive, heating to a feverish pitch that no amount of reasoning could deny. What had begun as a punishment became a subtle assault on her senses and she was no more capable of stopping him now than she had been all those years ago.

She didn't try. Lifting her arms, she gripped his neck to hold him closer, sliding her hands into his hair, feeling its strength and virility curling about her fingers. The roughness of his jawline abraded her skin, but she didn't care. She was totally absorbed with what he was doing to her and even breathing had become of less importance than the need to sustain that hungry kiss. His warmth, his maleness, his distinctive scent were all she cared about, and the heat that had started when he touched her spiralled down into her thighs.

She briefly acknowledged the risks she'd taken that morning when he'd attempted to make love to her at the hotel. When she'd taunted him, she'd thought she'd been in control; but she'd been wrong. If he'd ignored what she'd said, if he'd pinned her to the bed with his hard, muscled body as he was pinning her to her seat now, it would have been a different story. She couldn't control herself now and they were on a public car park, in full view of anyone who chose to walk by.

But, ultimately, it wasn't the fear of discovery that brought that passionate embrace to an end. It was the gear console between them that prevented Oliver from lifting her into his lap. It was an unrelenting barrier, and he swore as he was forced to accept defeat. And, as the world swam back into focus, Laura realised that once again she had had a lucky escape.

'We'll continue this later,' Oliver said darkly, but Laura was already regretting her own impulsive nature.

'Continue what?' she countered a little breathlessly, and felt a measure of satisfaction when Oliver jarred the gear as he started the car.

'Don't,' he warned her sharply, and she told herself it was only apprehension that caused the unfamiliar frisson of excitement in her stomach.

CHAPTER FOURTEEN

OLIVER stopped at another service area at lunchtime. He made a half-hearted attempt to swallow a ham sandwich and a can of soda while Laura tackled a tuna salad, but his stomach refused to accept the food, and, pushing his plate aside, he went and got himself another cola. He drank it, staring broodingly out of the diner's window at the traffic passing by on the road beneath them. He'd promised himself he wouldn't reopen his argument with Laura until he could be sure they wouldn't be interrupted, and he confined himself to comments about the weather—which was worsening—and the merits or otherwise of motorway food.

Laura answered him in monosyllables, but at least she said something, which was some relief. He'd been half afraid she'd revert to her earlier mood of outright opposition and ignore him completely.

It was dark by the time they crossed the Severn Bridge. A dull day had given way to an even duller late afternoon, and the rain spattering the windscreen was gaining in strength. Fortunately, they'd made good time to Port Talbot. The traffic had been light, but when they turned on to the road to Rhosmawr they hit the evening's rush hour. In consequence, it was almost seven o'clock when they reached the village.

He was aware that Laura was tenser now than she'd been for most of the journey, and he guessed that, like him, she was apprehensive about what they were going to find. The possibility that the thief—thieves?—might have vandalised the place was not appealing, although Oliver was sure Aunt Nell would have warned him if that had been the case. Whatever, as on the occasion when Griff had died, they were

156

both returning here in less than happy circumstances and Oliver, for one, would be glad when he knew the worst.

There was a car blocking the lane that led to the house and Oliver was forced to park behind it. It wasn't familiar, but that meant little. He didn't spend enough time at Penmadoc to recognise anyone's vehicle, but he did wonder if his mother had had another of her breakdowns and the doctor had had to be called out.

But that was uncharitable, he decided, aware of the irony in the thought. Being robbed was an unpleasant business, and Stella was unlikely to react to it any differently than anyone else. Besides, despite the incident of the phone call—which had acquired rather different connotations in his mind in any case—he had no real reason for doubting Stella's sincerity. Despite everything, surely even she would fight shy of actually shunning her own husband's funeral?

Or not.

'Your mother has visitors.'

Oliver grimaced. It was typical that the first words Laura had volunteered without encouragement should concern her stepmother.

He shrugged. 'Or your aunt does,' he countered, and felt her eyes flicker briefly in his direction.

'Oh, right,' she said, preparing to get out of the Jeep. 'Aunt Nell is a regular party animal.'

'One car does not constitute a party,' retorted Oliver, getting annoyed in spite of himself. He didn't want any reinforcement of his own doubts and his jaw compressed. Then, taking possession of the backpack, which she had stowed behind her seat, he pushed open his door. 'Wait here. I'll get an umbrella from the house.'

'I'm not made of sugar,' replied Laura, surrendering the backpack to him with evident reluctance. 'I won't melt.'

'Ain't that the truth,' muttered Oliver drily, but although he spoke in a barely audible tone he could tell by the way she glared at him that she'd heard what he'd said.

It had obviously been raining for some time because the ground underfoot was soft and muddy. It was an effort to keep his balance, and he felt a small smile curve his lips when he felt Laura clutch his coat to save herself. But he didn't say anything, and nor did she.

They tramped round to the back to save treading mud all through the house, and this time the outer door was unlocked. They both paused in the passage to remove their boots. It was easier for Oliver. He kicked off his without much effort. But Laura had to sit down on one of the wooden benches to unfasten her laces.

'Let me,' he said resignedly, brushing her cold hands aside, and although she would have obviously preferred to do it herself she didn't argue.

Oliver had half expected Aunt Nell to be waiting for them. But when they entered the kitchen the room was empty. Even the fire in the grate was in danger of dying, and Oliver used the iron poker to riddle the ash before adding a couple of logs to its smouldering embers.

'It's not like Aunt Nell to forget about it,' murmured Laura, clearly of the same mind as himself, and he nodded.

'Perhaps she's not feeling well,' he offered. 'It's possible that the shock of the break-in could have upset her and she's gone to bed.'

'Leaving the back door unlocked?' Laura arched her brows disbelievingly. 'I don't think so.'

'Then what's your solution?'

She shook her head. 'I don't have one.'

'Good. Nor do I.' Oliver gestured towards the door into the hall. 'Let's find Ma.'

'If she's here,' said Laura tightly, and Oliver gave her a retiring look.

'She's here,' he said, and somehow he knew that she was. Though why he was so sure, he didn't care to think.

The hall, too, offered no answers as to the whereabouts of the occupants of the house, and Oliver disliked the decidedly ominous feeling he was getting. Where the hell were they? he wondered impatiently. And why the devil didn't he just call his mother's name and let her tell him where she was?

There was no one in the dining room, the drawing room, or the library, but there was a light on in the study, and Oliver approached it with a feeling of apprehension. So far he'd seen no evidence of the break-in and he had the uneasy feeling that he was about to find out why. Laura was behind him as he pushed open the door and he sensed she was apprehensive, too, but once again the room was empty.

The picture which covered the door of the safe was in place, and Oliver swore. 'Dammit!' he exclaimed, stepping back into the hall and looking up the stairs. 'Is everyone in bed?'

Laura's lips parted. 'Are you sure it was Aunt Nell who phoned you last night?' she asked in a doubtful voice. 'I can't see that anything has been—'

'Disturbed?' Oliver's lips twisted. 'Yeah, I know. But it was Nell. I spoke to her this morning and she confirmed it.'

'So...' Laura shrugged. 'What should we do?'

'Find Ma,' said Oliver flatly, and without any more hesitation he started up the stairs.

Laura followed him. Even without looking, he was aware of her presence behind him, and the urge to tell her to stay downstairs was almost overwhelming. He didn't know what he was going to find, but something told him it wasn't going to be good.

But before they could reach the top of the stairs they heard voices. A man's voice at first, and then a woman's. Stella's.

'I tell you I did hear something,' the man insisted, and Oliver came to an abrupt halt.

'You're imagining things, Jaz.'

Stella sounded drowsy, and Oliver's heart skipped a beat.

'I don't think so. I heard voices,' the man asserted, and the increasing volume of his voice indicated that he had come out of the room. 'After what happened with Griff, we don't

want to risk getting caught again. God, Stell, it could be that
old woman. Perhaps she's brought someone back with her.'

Oliver didn't look at Laura but he knew exactly how she
must be feeling and he uttered an inward groan for the death
of his own hopes and expectations. Despite what had happened on the way here, he knew she wasn't indifferent to
him, but after this... He closed his eyes for a moment in
utter despair. She was never going to listen to him now.

'Nell's in Cardiff, I tell you.'

Stella had evidently come to join the man and Oliver heard
the sound of their footsteps approaching along the corridor
that led from his mother's room. There was a moment when
he considered going back down the stairs before they reached
the landing and discovered him, but although he knew Laura
wouldn't have stopped him he couldn't do it. He was fairly
sure it was for this reason that Nell had brought them here,
and while she couldn't have been sure that they'd come together she must have had a fairly good idea that they would.

'D'you want to leave this to me?' he asked in a low voice,
but Laura was staring white-faced down into the hall and he
wasn't sure that she'd even heard him. 'Laura,' he whispered,
lifting a hand and touching her cheek, wondering if this
would be the last time he'd ever lay a hand on her, and he
felt the effort it took for her to turn her head and look at him.

'Daddy,' she breathed, through dry lips. A wavering finger
pointed towards her father's study. 'I—I saw Daddy. He was
there.' She swallowed. 'In the doorway. Do you think he
turned on the light?'

The hairs rose on the back of Oliver's neck, and although
his common sense was telling him that she couldn't possibly
have seen her father something had evidently drained every
scrap of colour from her face.

'I—Laura—' he began helplessly, and then his mother
started to scream. The shrill sound was enough to banish any
intruder, ghostly or otherwise, and he saw, with some relief,
that Laura, too, was distracted by the sound.

'God!' It was the man, Jaz, who spoke first, and Oliver could even find it in his heart to feel sorry for him. Confronting his—what? Lover's?—son in only a pair of cotton boxers, while she shrieked like a banshee beside him, must be humiliating to say the least. 'I knew I'd heard something. Oh, hell—Stell, stop that horrible caterwauling, for God's sake.'

'Laura—Laura said she saw Griff,' she stammered, gathering a satin wrap around her, trying to get a hold on herself. 'In—in the doorway of the study. Oh, God, Jaz, do you think he was there?'

'Of course not.' Jaz gazed at her with impatient eyes. 'She's upset, that's all.' He grimaced. 'And who can blame her? I told you it was too soon to—to—'

'To what?' broke in Oliver coldly. 'To continue with your affair? God, Ma, you disgust me! And to think I believed that you were sincere.'

Stella pouted. 'What are you two doing here anyway?' She came down the stairs towards them. 'Don't be angry, Oliver. I've always needed affection, you know that.'

'Affection?' Oliver scoffed. 'This isn't affection!'

'Oh, and you'd know, of course.' His mother soon recovered her self-possession. 'You're so pure and untainted by sexual lusts yourself.'

'I'm disgusted because you were obviously conducting this affair right under Griff's nose,' snarled Oliver. 'I heard what your boyfriend said just now. You were here the afternoon Griff came back from hunting. He must have found you together. Was that why he had his heart attack?'

'No! No!' Stella was horrified. 'It wasn't like that.'

'What was it like, then?' Laura intervened, and Stella blinked rapidly before focussing on the younger woman. 'You phoned—*him*—' she indicated the older man '—the same night after you'd sworn you weren't fit enough to attend Daddy's funeral.'

Stella was taken aback. 'How do you know that?'

'She was there,' said Oliver flatly. 'Go on. I'm waiting to hear what happened the afternoon Griff died.'

Stella shook her head, clearly puzzled as to how Laura could have heard her call, but her son's expression forced her to continue. 'I—' She looked at her companion. 'I'm not sure what happened.'

'Oh, come on.' Oliver could feel his control slipping. 'You're not going to pretend that Griff didn't see you?'

'I don't know what he saw,' muttered Stella, wrapping her arms around herself.

'But he must have seen you,' said Laura unsteadily, and Jaz seemed to take pity on her.

'I heard something,' he admitted reluctantly. 'I told Stell we should have checked it out, but she said I was only imagining it.' He shrugged. 'She was obviously wrong.'

'*We* were wrong,' put in Stella, evidently not prepared to shoulder all the blame. She turned to her son. 'I tried to tell you how it was before the funeral. I'm a passionate woman, Oliver. I need—love.'

'What you need is sex,' Laura said tremulously, before Oliver could respond. 'Don't pretend Daddy didn't love you. He did. I only wish he'd never set eyes on you.'

'That's enough!' Stella was furious now. 'Don't you dare to talk to me in that holier-than-thou tone, because it won't wash, young lady.' A trembling finger was pointed at Laura. 'I know too much about you. I always have. That was why you took every chance you could to tell tales about me to your father; why you poisoned Griff's mind against me—'

'That's not true!' Laura's voice was trembling, but Stella didn't seem to care.

'How do you think your precious father would have felt if he'd known what you were really like?' she demanded contemptuously. 'He thought you were such a good little girl. That butter wouldn't melt in your mouth.'

'For God's sake, Ma—'

'No, why shouldn't I defend myself?' Stella exclaimed,

shaking off her son's attempt to restrain her. 'She was eager enough to tell me what she thought of me.'

'For pity's sake, Stella—'

Jaz appealed to her, but she ignored him. 'I've waited a long time to say this, Oliver,' she declared. 'I won't let her get away with it.'

'This isn't going to change anything, Ma—'

'Isn't it? Isn't it?' She held up her head. 'You don't know the half of it. You don't know why she really came to your room, what she'd planned—'

'Planned?' Oliver was frankly scathing. 'For God's sake, Ma, stop while you've still got a shred of decency left.'

'You don't understand.' Swallowing convulsively, Stella pressed a trembling hand to his chest. 'You think I'm just making these things up to defend myself, but it's not true. She wanted you, Oliver, and she was prepared to do anything to get you.'

'No—'

Laura's cry almost went unnoticed, but Oliver had heard it, and, putting his hands on his mother's shoulders, he said flatly, 'Let's leave Laura out of this, shall we? I know you've never liked her. You've made that plain enough, God knows.' He glanced at Laura's white face. 'But it's been fourteen years since that night. We've got over it. We've moved on—'

'She hasn't.' Stella turned to point at her stepdaughter once again. 'She still hates me. She always has.'

Oliver groaned. 'You're not going to get away with this, Ma.' He took a deep breath. 'Now, I think we've established that Griff saw or heard—something when he got back that afternoon. I assume that accounts for the fact that it was two hours before you found—found him?'

'That's right.' Jaz nodded. 'Stell was nearly frantic when she found the body. But it was too late. There was nothing we could do.'

'Except hide what had really happened,' said Oliver bitterly. 'My God, Ma, how could you live with yourself?'

'Don't preach to me about living with myself,' retorted his mother savagely. 'At least I've never had to get myself pregnant to try and hold on to a man.'

There was absolute silence after this revelation. Even the house was still, as if even inanimate objects sensed that any sound would be a desecration. Oliver didn't move. He couldn't. For a few moments the actual portent of his mother's words had him stunned and frozen to the spot.

Then, with an anguished sound, Laura broke the death-like stillness. Whirling, she turned and ran back down the stairs, and as Oliver watched her go so many things suddenly made sense to him. God, he thought, his brain stumbling slowly back into gear. She had been pregnant when he went away. She had been expecting his baby, and he'd known nothing about it.

But before he could go after her Stella seemed to realise she'd made a fatal mistake. In her efforts to discredit Laura, she had inadvertently told her son something that it was not in her best interests to reveal.

'Oh, Oliver,' she said, reaching for his arm. 'I'm so sorry. You were never meant to hear about this. Especially not from me.'

Oliver shook her off, dragging his eyes away from the stairs down which Laura had just vanished with an effort. 'What?'

'The fact that she was pregnant,' Stella prompted him urgently. 'That's what she'd intended all along. Don't you see? It was her way of getting back at me—at both of us—for my marrying her father. Thank heavens nothing came of it. It would have ruined your life—all our lives.'

Oliver stared at her disbelievingly. 'You're crazy!' He blinked. 'And what did you mean? Nothing came of it?' His blood chilled. 'Did she have the child?'

'Of course not.' Stella was impatient.

'So she—what? Miscarried?' Right now, Oliver didn't know which was worse.

'Yes, she lost it,' said his mother irritably. 'Honestly, Oliver, I would have thought—'

'That's the trouble,' said Oliver heavily. 'You don't think. You never have.'

'The safe's been opened.'

Laura spoke from the foot of the stairs, successfully putting an end to their discussion, and Stella started to protest behind him.

'How does she know?' she cried, but Oliver wasn't listening to her.

'I'm coming,' he said instead, and hurried down the stairs to where Laura was waiting. 'Perhaps there has been a robbery, after all.'

'A robbery?'

His mother hurried after him, and he wondered if she was as much in the dark as he was himself. 'The break-in,' he said, as he reached Laura. 'Aunt Nell phoned me last night. She said someone had attempted to break in.'

Stella's eyes flashed. 'There was no break-in!' she exclaimed, but she was forced to follow her son and her stepdaughter across the hall and into the study, however unwilling she might have been. She stared mutinously at the open safe that Laura must have found when she'd removed the picture. 'If Nell told you there was a break-in, she was trying to cause trouble, by the sound of it.' She scowled. 'I opened the safe.'

'You opened it?' Oliver's lips tightened. 'How? You didn't have a key.'

Stella coloured. 'If you must know, I had a copy of the key made before Griff died. It's hardly Fort Knox. A child could have opened it.'

Oliver looked at Laura. She had no idea what he was thinking, and he knew the time had come when he had to climb down from the fence. 'So what did you find?' he asked, knowing full well his mother would know what he was saying. He crossed to the safe and removed the handful of papers and documents he found there. 'There's nothing much here. Just a few old bank statements—' He paused, and then drew an envelope from his pocket. 'I wonder—were you looking for this?'

It was the will and Stella's consternation was plain. 'I knew you had to have it with you when it wasn't there, but you can't—you can't—'

Stella was almost beside herself, but it was Laura who was looking puzzled now. 'A will?' she exclaimed blankly. 'Did Daddy keep a copy of his will in the safe?'

'Not this will,' Oliver told her heavily. 'This isn't the will he'd deposited with Marcus Venning, I'm afraid. This is his new will. It was made fairly recently. My mother found it before the funeral, you see.'

Laura blinked. 'Then why didn't she—?'

'She naturally assumed it was the same will that Marcus had witnessed. It wasn't until the will was read that she realised her mistake. And by then she didn't want to admit she'd found it, particularly as the old will was so much more favourable to her.'

Laura hesitated. 'The terms of the new will are different?' she asked faintly, and Oliver realised she still didn't understand what it might mean.

'They are,' he said gently. 'Penmadoc is left to you entirely. My mother—' He gave Stella a scathing glance. 'My mother is quite adequately taken care of, but your father obviously wanted you to have the house.'

'And you've had this will all along?'

Laura was evidently making sense of what he'd said, and Oliver felt his spirits sink to the floor. 'Since I went back to London, yes,' he said, ignoring Stella's scowling face. 'I took the safe key, too. I had no idea my mother had a copy.'

'You had no right to take the will,' began Stella angrily, but this time Jaz, who had halted in the doorway, chose to intervene.

'Leave it, Stell,' he said. 'Laura knows about it now, so

there's no good in labouring the point. I told you that Oliver would never stand for it, but you wouldn't listen to me.'

'Well, I'll never forgive him for this,' choked Stella tearfully, but Oliver sensed they were tears of anger, not of distress. He'd never forgive himself, but for an entirely different reason. In even listening to his mother, he had probably destroyed any chance of Laura's trusting in him again.

'I can't believe it.' Laura was shaking. 'So that's why Stella didn't want to attend Daddy's funeral. She was putting off the reading of the will—why? Because she thought I'd put her out of the house?'

'Yeah.' Oliver nodded. 'And I didn't say anything, even when Marcus read the old will,' he added, condemning himself completely. 'I wanted to talk to you first, but you disappeared before I got the chance. Then this morning—' But he didn't want to go into that, not in this company. 'She is my mother, for my sins. I guess I didn't want to be responsible for driving her out of her home.'

'I—I can understand that.' Laura was more charitable than he would have given her credit for. But Stella wanted nothing from her.

'Just listen to her,' she said. 'Miss Prim and Proper! You weren't so prim and proper when you were crawling into my son's bed!'

Laura blanched, and Oliver had heard enough. 'Shut it, Ma!' he exclaimed savagely. 'I still don't think you have any idea what you've done. Without you, Laura and I might still have been together. You ruined my life. You've ruined all our lives. I'll never forgive you for that.'

CHAPTER FIFTEEN

LAURA sat at the window of her apartment in Greenwich Village, gazing out at the plane trees in the park across the street. It was early evening and the park was practically deserted now, the children and their carers who had occupied the swings and fed the ducks on the ornamental pond were long gone, and twilight crept like a violet wraith across the grass.

Laura sipped at the cup of coffee in her hand. Despite its beauty, this was the time of day she liked least. Evening heralded the night and she was still sleeping badly. She often spent the early hours of the morning reading some would-be author's manuscript, and she'd threatened Matt that she was going to bill him for all those extra hours.

Of course, she wouldn't. Since her return from Wales almost four months ago, her employer had been particularly nice to her, and although she suspected it was because he didn't want to lose her it was good to feel needed.

By someone.

She took a deep breath and fought back the wave of anxiety that swept over her. She had nothing to be anxious about. Not really. It wasn't as if she hadn't been in this situation before, and she'd coped then. She could cope now. What had changed, after all? Nothing. And she'd been a fool to even imagine that it might.

All the same, the knowledge of the phone call she'd made three days ago weighed heavily on her conscience. She'd known at the time she was dialling Oliver's number that she was probably making another stupid mistake, but that hadn't stopped her from going through with it. She'd needed to speak to him; she'd needed closure, she'd told herself, if that

was what it achieved. She couldn't go on living in this vac-
uum of emotion, not knowing what, if anything, she might
have rescued from the wreck she'd made of her life.

Predictably, perhaps, Oliver hadn't been at home when
she'd rung. His man, Thomas, had explained that he was in
Spain taking pictures of bulls and bullrings for an exhibition
of Spanish culture that was to be shown in London later in
the year. When he'd asked her if she had any message she
would like him to pass along, she'd demurred. 'It wasn't
important,' she'd assured him firmly, and then burst into tears
as soon as she'd put down the phone.

Which seemed to prove that she hadn't got over Oliver,
after all. And that was the real reason she was feeling so
anxious now. How long was it going to take for her to start
feeling in control again? How long before she stopped scanning every newspaper, North American and English, for
some word of him? How long before her life resumed its
normal pattern and she could start feeling whole again?

For ever?

She expelled a rueful breath. Of course, if she hadn't been
scanning the papers so avidly, she might have missed the
article about Natalie, she consoled herself. At least now she
didn't have to picture him and the beautiful model together.
They had apparently split and Natalie was now engaged to
be married to a Greek shipping tycoon. It must have been a
whirlwind courtship, Laura reflected, unless Oliver and
Natalie had broken up as soon as she'd returned to the States.

It was possible, she supposed. After the things Oliver had
said, it would have been hypocritical of him to pretend that
he and Natalie had a future together. But then, he had said a
lot of things, most of which had gone over her head, and in
the aftermath of learning of Stella's betrayal Laura had found
it difficult to take anything in.

That night—the night the truth had come out—didn't seem
quite real now. Stella's affair with Dilys James's husband—
that was who she'd been phoning after the funeral, not

Dilys—her father's death; the duplicity over the second will; —it all seemed totally remote from her life here in New York. It was as if it had all happened to someone else and even now, four months on, she couldn't quite believe it.

Perhaps that was why she'd been so willing to take the easy way out and return to the United States. Life was so much less complicated here and certainly Matt had been glad to see her back. He wasn't interested in what her stepmother had done, or who owned Penmadoc. As far as he was concerned, she had a job to do, and if she didn't want to do it he'd find someone who would.

Not that anyone else had attempted to change her mind. Apart from informing Marcus Venning that a new will had been found—and Oliver had done that—her contribution to events had been minimal. Despite his offer to take responsibility for what had happened, Laura had had no desire to take legal proceedings against either Oliver or his mother, and a story had been concocted as to why the will hadn't been discovered before now. The fact that it had involved a missing key was something of an irony; but Marcus Venning was more concerned that her father should have felt the need to approach some obscure firm of solicitors in London, rather than admitting his personal grief to him, and hadn't probed too deeply into their explanation.

Stella had left Penmadoc the morning after the scene in the study. With Jaz James's help, she'd moved into a flat in Rhosmawr and, as far as Laura was aware, she was still there. Whether the affair would survive recent events was anyone's guess. Stella had expected to inherit Penmadoc and with the sale of the house behind her she would have been a very wealthy woman. As it was, she was just another widow, living on a pension, and if that pension was rather more generous than most it was still considerably less than Jaz must have anticipated.

Laura's lips flattened against her teeth. Her heart ached for what her father must have suffered in the months before he died. He'd obviously known Stella was being unfaithful to him, ergo the new will, but finding her with another man in his own house must have been the last straw.

Of course, it was always possible that his heart attack would have happened anyway. In her more charitable moments, Laura hoped that this was so. It made it a little easier to try and forgive her stepmother—although she knew she would never forget.

As far as her own psychic experiences were concerned, she was rather less certain. Although she thought she knew what she'd seen, she had to accept that she'd been in a particularly receptive mood, and the mind could play tricks on the eye. Of course, if she'd still been alive, her grandmother would have believed her, but the old lady had always been looking for evidence of second sight in her offspring. Whatever, Laura was sure she hadn't imagined the change of atmosphere in the house after Stella had departed. Maybe there were such things as restless spirits, after all.

It had been agreed that Aunt Nell should continue to live at Penmadoc. Laura had given her aunt power of attorney to act in her absence, which meant the old lady wouldn't have to apply to her for funds for the day-to-day running of the house. It suited Laura that way. Much as she loved the place, it would be a long time before she'd be able to face the thought of living there again.

Oliver had left for London as soon as the formalities had been dealt with. To get back to Natalie, she'd assumed, though subsequent events had cast doubt on that supposition. Whatever, he hadn't seemed inclined to offer any explanation, and she'd left for New York without speaking to him privately again.

She had wondered if he might try to get in touch with her. Aunt Nell had her address and she'd left instructions that, should he ask for it, her aunt should feel free to pass it on. But she'd been back for almost four months now and it seemed that, as far as Oliver was concerned, she might as well have dropped off the roof of the world.

Then she'd read the article about Natalie.

At first, she'd decided it was nothing to do with her. As far as she knew, Oliver could be heartbroken over the severing of his relationship with the fashion model and any intervention on her part might be construed as interference. But then she'd started remembering the things he'd said to his mother that night in her father's study and her spirits had taken a distinctly upward turn.

After all, it was possible that Oliver thought she didn't want to talk to him. She'd given him very little encouragement to believe she'd be willing to listen to anything he had to say. After that scene in her hotel room and what had happened on the journey to Penmadoc, he must have felt he was fighting a losing battle with the past.

That was why she'd made that phone call. Straight away, so that she'd had no time to have second thoughts. But— Oliver hadn't been available. He'd been too busy getting on with his life, and if she had any sense she'd do the same.

A cab cruised along the street below her. It was moving slowly as if the driver—or his passenger—was scanning the numbers on the buildings, looking for a particular address. It slowed outside the warehouse, above which she had her loft apartment, and then moved on down the street. The momentary thrill she'd felt at the prospect of a visitor quickly dissipated. Who was likely to come and see her? She blew out a tired breath. She really would have to get herself a life.

The cab was coming back. Laura guessed the driver had unloaded his passenger and was hoping to pick up another fare to take back to Manhattan. But, to her astonishment, the cab stopped right outside her building and the rear door was thrust open to allow a man to get out.

Oliver!

Laura scrambled up from the banquette, almost spilling her coffee in her efforts to get away from the window. That was all she needed: for him to see her sitting there like some sad waif waiting for someone to notice her. She was supposed to be living the good life in New York. What was he going to think if he found her spending a lonely evening dwelling on the events of the past?

Did she care?

She inched back towards the window, using the silk drapes as a screen between her and what was going on outside. Oliver had evidently paid the driver because the cab was some distance away now, and she drew a sharp breath when she thought for a moment that Oliver had gone with him. But then he stepped back from under the overhang and looked up at her windows, and she realised he was probably trying to gauge if she was at home.

She could pretend to be out.

Drawing back, she gave the thought only a momentary consideration. What would be the point of that? she asked herself scornfully. Was her pride so great she was prepared to gamble on the chance of him coming back?

No!

As the doorbell rang, she was already hastening across the wide expanse of the living area, depositing her coffee cup on the breakfast bar, opening the door that led to the stairs. A steep flight led down to the outer door which, in common with most doors in New York, was fairly heavily secured.

For once, she didn't attempt to identify her caller before opening the door, and she took an involuntary gulp of air when she pulled it inwards and found Oliver waiting outside. He looked so beloved, so familiar. It took an actual effort to merely stand aside and invite him to come in.

'Hi,' he said, evidently feeling some greeting was necessary, and Laura managed a faint smile as she closed the door behind him.

'Hi,' she said a little huskily. 'Do you want to come up?'

Oliver took a deep breath. 'Why not?' he said, stepping back and indicating the stairs. 'After you.'

Laura would have preferred to follow him. In dark trousers and a matching V-necked sweater, he looked good from any angle, while she was acutely conscious of the definite drawbacks of short dungarees and bare feet.

But being bashful now wasn't going to get her anywhere, and, taking her courage in both hands, she hastened up the stairs in front of him.

He paused in the doorway to her apartment and looked around. The huge space had been divided into areas for living and cooking and sleeping, with the bathroom concealed behind opaque glass walls. Laura was quite proud of the way she'd furnished it, and the overall effect was one of lightness and comfort. Despite its size, underfloor heating could cope with the lowest temperatures, but this evening the windows were open and the breeze that rippled the rose-pink curtains brought the scent of the flowers that grew in the park across the way into the room.

Laura halted in the middle of the Chinese rug that defined the living area. Her knees felt decidedly shaky, and she would have liked nothing better than to curl up on the ivory velvet sofa, but until she knew why Oliver was here she knew she'd never be able to sit still.

'Impressive,' he said at last, coming into the apartment and closing the door. He glanced up at the wide skylight. 'This would be a great place to have a studio.'

'I suppose it would.' Laura wondered if he was as nervous as she was, and then decided he couldn't be. If he were, he wouldn't be wasting time talking about her apartment. Or would he? 'You'd know more about that than me.'

'Yeah.' Oliver's lips tightened for a moment. 'Yeah, I guess that's one thing I do know about.'

Laura forced a smile. 'You're too modest.'

'Am I?' He shrugged. 'I wouldn't put money on it.'

Laura asked, 'Can I—can I get you anything? Some coffee? A drink?'

'Do you have anything alcoholic?'

'I think so.' Moving round him, Laura hurried into the small kitchen and opened the fridge. 'Is a German beer okay?'

'Anything,' said Oliver, crossing the rug to the window. 'Nice view.'

'I like it.' Laura hesitated over whether to offer him a glass and then decided she was being too formal. She came out of the kitchen again and held out the bottle. 'There you go.'

'Thanks.'

He came away from the window to take the bottle from her and their fingers touched. Laura drew her hand away immediately but she couldn't stop her gaze from darting to his face. It was the first time she'd looked into his eyes since he'd come into the apartment and her breath caught at the instant awareness that leapt between them. It was as if something hot and heavy had entered the air and for a moment it was difficult to breathe.

'Why did you phone?'

He spoke roughly, as if the words had been dragged out of him, and Laura wished she'd thought to pick up her cup of coffee in passing, to give her hands something to do.

'Why—why did I phone?' she echoed, her fingers opening and closing below the denim hems of her dungarees. She turned the question back on him. 'Why—why do you think I phoned?'

'Oh, no.' Oliver swallowed a mouthful of his beer before regarding her impatiently. 'I asked first.' He took a deep breath. 'Is something wrong?'

Laura's jaw was in danger of dropping, but she managed to control it. 'What could be wrong?' she countered. 'Did— did Thomas tell you I'd said that something was wrong?'

Oliver closed his eyes for a moment and then opened them again to give her a weary look. 'Why are you doing this, Laura?' he asked. 'It's a simple question. I want to know why you rang. What's the matter? Do you wish you hadn't?'

'No!' She swallowed. 'No, of course not.'

'Then why did you ring?' he persisted. 'I—have to know. I *need* to know.' He heaved a sigh. 'Can't you tell me if I've made another stupid mistake by coming here?'

Laura's tongue circled her upper lip. 'You haven't,' she said swiftly. Then, before she could lose her nerve, she added, 'I—I'm glad you came.'

'Are you?'

He didn't sound as if he believed her and she hurried to reassure him. 'Yes. Yes, I am. I wanted to see you.' She paused, half afraid that she was presuming too much. 'I—I wanted to tell you how sorry I was when I read about—about you and Natalie.'

Incredulity entered his features now. 'Me and Natalie?' he echoed disbelievingly. 'You're not serious.'

'Why not?' Laura endeavoured to sound convincing. 'I read about her engagement to some Greek ship owner in the newspaper.' She lifted her shoulders. 'You split up.'

Oliver stared at her for a long moment and then raised the bottle to his lips again. She watched the strong muscles of his throat work as he drank the cold beer and then flinched when he lowered the bottle and turned a contemptuous gaze on her.

'You phoned to commiserate with me about Natalie?' he said harshly. 'Gee, thanks.'

Laura quivered. 'Don't speak to me like that. I didn't know how you'd feel about it.'

'Didn't you? Didn't you?' He almost sounded as if he blamed her for the break-up. 'Get real, Laura. You knew exactly how I'd feel about it.'

'But I don't.' The words were wrung from her, and she thrust her hands into the pockets of her dungarees to hide their agitation from him. 'I don't know anything.'

Oliver's mouth compressed and he turned, very slowly, and deposited the bottle on the window seat behind him. Then, turning back, he said flatly, 'I'm supposed to believe that?'

'Yes. Yes.'

'Well, what the hell do you think I'm doing here?' he demanded, and she realised that although she'd thought he looked much the same as usual there were distinct hollows beneath his eyes.

But she couldn't mention them, not when he was waiting for an answer, and, curling her fists into balls, she said, 'I don't know, do I? Maybe you've got an assignment in New York. Maybe you thought you'd just—look me up.'

'Oh, right.' Oliver shook his head. 'That would have been convenient, wouldn't it? An assignment in New York turning up just three days after your call?'

'It could have happened,' she protested, and he gave her a disparaging look.

'No, it couldn't,' he said harshly. 'I was in Seville—should still be in Seville, if everybody had their rights. But I'm not.'

Laura stared at him. 'You—you came back—for me?'

'Yes, I came back for you,' he said impatiently. 'For God's sake, Laura, I thought something must have happened—' He broke off wearily. 'I thought you needed me.'

'Oh, I do.'

Laura's cry was heartfelt, and Oliver gazed at her with tormented eyes. 'Do you mean that?' he asked hoarsely, and she knew she couldn't prevaricate any longer.

'Yes. Yes, I mean it,' she said huskily, reaching for him, and with a muffled oath Oliver captured her hands with his.

'God, Laura,' he said, taking her hands behind his back, bringing her close to his lean, muscled body. 'Do you like putting me through this kind of torture?' His mouth nuzzled her cheek. 'Don't you think I've suffered enough?'

Laura couldn't speak. For so long she'd accepted that anything there might have been between her and Oliver had been destroyed by his mother's treachery. Even knowing that he'd wanted to make love to her when they were in London hadn't been enough to breach all those years of pain and humiliation when she'd believed that the love they'd shared had meant as little to him as his mother had said. But, suddenly, anything was possible, and when his mouth first nudged and then took possession of hers she had no hesitation in arching against him and parting her lips for his kiss.

When his hands came to cradle her neck, hers slipped beneath his sweater, finding the warm curve of his spine. His skin, smooth and warm, seemed to welcome her caress, and the sound he made against her mouth convinced her that this time she was doing something right.

Meanwhile, his kiss was melting any remaining inhibitions. It hardly seemed possible that just a few minutes ago she had been despairing of the emptiness of her life. His tongue, his lips, the sensual pressure she could feel against her stomach were pouring heat and colour into her soul. She felt dazed; enchanted; blessed; granted the second chance she'd never dreamed might be hers.

'I was scared, you know,' he muttered, releasing her mouth to seek the scented hollow of her throat. 'All the way over on the plane, I kept telling myself I was taking one hell of a chance, that I had no real proof that you wanted to see me, that you might not simply have wanted to talk...'

'To talk?' Laura's voice was scratchy. 'What about?'

'You tell me.' Oliver's hands curved over her shoulders, sliding the straps of her dungarees aside. The cropped top she was wearing underneath exposed a satisfying width of her midriff, and she felt the loose denim sliding down her legs. 'How about Natalie?' he suggested, his breathing unmistakably quickening. 'Do you need me to tell you that from the minute I saw you again there was no room in my life for anyone else?'

Laura's nod was shaky. 'Yes,' she said definitely. 'Yes, I need you to tell me that.'

'Okay.' Oliver's fingers insinuated themselves into the top of her bikini briefs. 'So I've told you.' He caught his breath as his hands cupped her bare bottom. 'Anything else?'

Laura trembled. 'Did—did you mean what you said that night at Penmadoc?'

Oliver groaned. 'Yes, I meant it,' he muttered, parting his legs to bring her even closer against him. 'I meant everything I've ever said to you, baby. I love you. I guess I always have. I was just too stupid to do anything about it before now.'

For the first time, Laura appreciated the advantage of her bed being just at the other side of the loft. A colonial four-poster, it was easily big enough to accommodate Oliver's greater length, and after he'd deposited her on the rose satin coverlet she took great pleasure in watching him strip off his clothes.

It had been almost fifteen years since they'd first made love, but Oliver had hardly changed at all, she thought, hugging herself. He was still strong and muscular, and if the years had added maturity that was only to be expected. His chest was broader than she remembered, perhaps, and his stomach was flatter, but the powerful thickness of his manhood still rose proudly from its nest of coarse dark hair.

She'd watched him that day at the hotel, of course. But then she'd believed his only intention was to humiliate her, and that was why she'd done her best to humiliate him. She hadn't succeeded. She'd only succeeded in embarrassing herself; in proving once and for all that where Oliver was concerned she had no real resistance at all.

'Hey.' Oliver saw her watching him. 'Am I the only one getting naked around here?'

Laura caught her breath. 'No,' she conceded, using her crossed arms to haul her cotton top over her head. But when it came to loosening her bra her hands stilled.

'Don't be shy with me,' he said gently, coming down on to the bed beside her and moving her hands aside. With enviable skill, he released the front fastening of the lacy garment, and then sucked in a breath. 'There: that's better.'

Laura's face flamed with colour as he bore her back against the pillows, and panic, plain and simple, made her tremble as if this were her first time. And it was, in a way, she thought unsteadily, as his fingers hooked the hem of her briefs and tugged them off. Her experiences with Conor had hardly been earth-shattering, and towards the end of their marriage they'd barely spoken, let alone anything else.

She was half afraid she wouldn't know what to do, what to say, how to please him, but she needn't have worried. With Oliver, everything had always been instinctive somehow, and his hands and lips made a nonsense of her fears. With only a touch, he was able to arouse her deepest needs, her deepest feelings, and she gave up worrying about anything but the pleasure he was so effortlessly bestowing.

His hands skimmed her breasts, teasing the taut peaks with his palms, before replacing one of his hands with his tongue. He rolled the swollen nipple between his tongue and his teeth, and then dragged it into his mouth to suckle on the tip.

Both breasts received this sensuous attention before he trailed kisses over her stomach and midriff, exploring the dark hollow of her navel, nudging the red-gold curls that hid her femininity. One long finger discovered her moist readiness, and although she didn't want to expose her eagerness she couldn't help arching up against that sensual invasion.

'Oh, baby,' he said thickly, 'me, too.' And, easing himself between her splayed legs, he joined his body to hers.

'God, you have no idea how much I've wanted this,' he added as she reached for him. 'How much I've wanted to be buried deep inside you, so deep that we don't know where you end and I begin.'

'I love you, Oliver,' she breathed, her chest constricted by the ache of emotion that seemed to be filling her. 'Oh, Oliver, I love you so much.'

Some time later, Laura opened her eyes, to find Oliver propped on one elbow beside her, watching her. For a moment, she was too embarrassed to say anything, and, as if sensing her confusion, Oliver bent his head to kiss her lips.

'Mmm, you taste as sweet as you look—and I should

know,' he murmured, reminding her that he hadn't been satisfied with making love with her just once. There'd been a
second time, when he'd brought her to the brink of fulfilment
with his tongue, before his own needs had demanded a fuller
demonstration of his love for her.

'You shouldn't say things like that,' she said now, her
cheeks brimming with becoming colour. 'Isn't it enough that
you've reduced me to a trembling supplicant at your hands?'

'Well, hell, lady, join the club,' he teased her softly. 'And
I reckon I've earned the right to tell you I love you any way
I choose, don't you?'

Laura pressed her lips together. 'I—I suppose so.'

'You suppose so?'

'All right.' She dimpled. 'All right, yes. So long as I can
do the same.'

'Hey, you can say what you like to me,' he assured her.
'So long as you're prepared to take the consequences.'

'What consequences?'

A trailing hand cupped her breast. 'Do you want me to
show you?'

'I—no.' With some regret, Laura declined. 'I—I think we
should talk about the consequences of—of what—this means
first.'

Oliver sighed. 'You mean us?' He gave her a wary look.
'I should have thought that was obvious.'

'Is it?' Laura was nervous.

'I hope so.' His eyes darkened. 'I assumed—I hoped—it
meant that we were going to be together from now on. I
mean,' he hastened on, 'I'm not suggesting you should give
up your life here if that's what you want. I'm quite prepared
to relocate, if that would please you.'

'Please me?' Laura felt the tears sliding down her cheeks
but she couldn't help it. 'You please me,' she said, lifting
her hand to cup his face. 'So—so very much.'

Oliver's eyes softened. 'Well, then—'

'There are other—other things we have to talk about.'

'What other things?' He closed his eyes for a moment. 'Oh, you mean the baby.' He groaned. 'Dear God, if I'd known—'

'I don't mean the baby,' she told him softly. 'Losing it was terrible, but, believe me, it was nothing compared to losing you.'

'Oh, sweetheart—'

'No, let me finish. I want you to know I don't blame you for anything any more. We were both too young, I realise that now. In that, at least, your mother was right—'

'My mother—'

'Yes, your mother,' agreed Laura huskily. 'She's not going to be pleased about—about us.'

'And that worries you?'

Laura nodded. 'A little.'

'Well, don't let it.' Oliver drew her closer. 'If and when my mother decides she has anything more to say to me, she'll say it in my time, not hers, and she knows that.' He paused. 'She and I have come to an understanding since you left Penmadoc. She doesn't interfere in my life and I don't interfere in hers.' His lips twisted. 'Of course, she was sure you would never speak to me again, and until Thomas rang me in Spain and told me about your call I'm afraid I was inclined to believe her.'

'Oh, Oliver...'

She reached up and bestowed a warm kiss at the corner of his mouth and he pulled a wry face. 'It's true. I guess I've been as guilty of listening to her lies as anyone. But, I have to admit, in this instance, I thought she'd got it right.'

'How could you think that?'

Laura was appalled, and Oliver hastened to explain. 'I was sure you'd try to see me again before you left for the States. This assignment I was on in Spain is already way behind schedule because I hung about for so long, waiting for you to contact me.'

'But you left Penmadoc,' protested Laura. 'As soon as

you'd arranged things with Mr Venning, you cleared off back to London. To Natalie, I assumed. Why else?'

'Try imagining how I was feeling,' Oliver said simply. 'Between us—my mother and I—we'd really mucked up your life. I was sure you'd never believe anything I had to say again.'

Laura shook her head. 'And I thought you were only using me to prove to yourself that I'd never got over you.'

'I wish.'

'Do you?' She looked up at him with guarded eyes.

'That you'd never got over me?' said Oliver ruefully. 'Of course I do. I'm only human.'

Laura caught her lower lip between her teeth. 'I wish I'd known.'

'Why?' He gazed intently at her. 'I thought you hated me—for a while, at least.'

'I never hated you,' said Laura honestly. 'I resented you; I resented the way you could hurt me. But I never hated you.'

Oliver frowned. 'But when you married Neill—'

'I should never have married Conor.' She sighed. 'I knew that when you came home for the wedding. I guess I was hoping I could get you out from under my skin. Trying to prove to myself that I didn't care you'd made a success of your life without me.'

'Hey...' Oliver's knuckles brushed the dampness from her cheeks. 'Being good at what I do doesn't mean I've made a success of my life.' He grimaced. 'These last few months I've realised that I've spent all these years searching for something I had and lost. You. Everything else is unimportant.'

'You don't mean that.'

'Don't I?' His thumb skimmed her breast. 'Well, I suppose I am proud of some of my work, but it means very little if you've no one to share it with.' He nuzzled her throat. 'I want to share it with you, Laura. Only you.' He drew back to look at her. 'Will you marry me?'

'Marry you?' Laura's lips parted. 'Oh, Oliver—'

'No, wait.' He seemed to think she was about to refuse, and he hurried on, 'I know your job's important to you—

'Oliver—'

'—and, as I said before, if you'd prefer to stay in New York, I'm quite prepared to live here.'

'Oliver, listen to me—'

'I don't know how Thomas will take it, of course. But we can face that hurdle when we come to it. So long as we're together—'

'Yes, so long as we're together,' broke in Laura breathlessly. 'Darling Oliver, of course I'll marry you, and I'll live any place you like.'

He looked stunned. 'You will?' he exclaimed, and then pulled her into his arms and buried his mouth on hers. Hot passion flared between them once again, but on this occasion he tried to keep his head. 'And—and your work?'

'I've thought about it,' admitted Laura softly. 'I've already discussed working at home with Conor's uncle Matt because I fully intended to return to my roots one day. I had thought I'd stay with Aunt Nell at Penmadoc, but I'd much prefer to stay in London with you.' She smiled. 'We could even keep this place as an extra studio. It might be nice to come here sometimes and remember tonight.'

'You mean it?'

Oliver was delighted and Laura wound her arms around his neck. 'Well, one day we might go back to Penmadoc. I want to have your baby, and the air there is much better than in the town.'

'As long as we're together,' he echoed softly. 'I never want to risk losing you again.'

Three magnificent millionaires from Down Under—
it's high time they were married!

Meet Tyler, Harry and Val...

The Australian Playboys

in Miranda Lee's racy, sexy new
three-part series.

THE PLAYBOY'S PROPOSITION
#2128

THE PLAYBOY'S VIRGIN
#2134

THE PLAYBOY IN PURSUIT
#2140

Available in September, October and November in
Harlequin Presents® wherever Harlequin books are sold.

You're not going to believe this offer!

**In October and November 2000, buy any two Harlequin
or Silhouette books and save $10.00 off future purchases,
or buy any three and save $20.00 off future purchases!**

Just fill out this form and attach 2 proofs of purchase (cash register
receipts) from October and November 2000 books and Harlequin will
send you a coupon booklet worth a total savings of $10.00 off future
purchases of Harlequin and Silhouette books in 2001. Send us 3 proofs
of purchase and we will send you a coupon booklet worth a total
savings of $20.00 off future purchases.

Saving money has never been this easy.

I accept your offer! Please send me a coupon booklet:

Name: _____

Address: _____ City: _____

State/Prov.: _____ Zip/Postal Code: _____

Optional Survey!

In a typical month, how many Harlequin or Silhouette books would you buy <u>new</u> at retail stores?

☐ Less than 1   ☐ 1   ☐ 2   ☐ 3 to 4   ☐ 5+

Which of the following statements best describes how you <u>buy</u> Harlequin or Silhouette books?
Choose one answer only that <u>best</u> describes you.

☐ I am a regular buyer and reader
☐ I am a regular reader but buy only occasionally
☐ I only buy and read for specific times of the year, e.g. vacations
☐ I subscribe through Reader Service but also buy at retail stores
☐ I mainly borrow and buy only occasionally
☐ I am an occasional buyer and reader

Which of the following statements best describes how you <u>choose</u> the Harlequin and Silhouette
series books you buy <u>new</u> at retail stores? By "series," we mean books within a particular line,
such as *Harlequin PRESENTS* or *Silhouette SPECIAL EDITION*. Choose one answer only that
<u>best</u> describes you.

☐ I only buy books from my favorite series
☐ I generally buy books from my favorite series but also buy
   books from other series on occasion
☐ I buy some books from my favorite series but also buy from
   many other series regularly
☐ I buy all types of books depending on my mood and what
   I find interesting and have no favorite series

Please send this form, along with your cash register receipts as proofs of purchase, to:
In the U.S.: Harlequin Books, P.O. Box 9057, Buffalo, NY 14269
In Canada: Harlequin Books, P.O. Box 622, Fort Erie, Ontario L2A 5X3
(Allow 4-6 weeks for delivery) Offer expires December 31, 2000.   PHQ4002

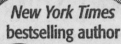